Harry Potter & FANTASTIC BEASTS

A SPELLBINDING GUIDE to the FILMS

BY MICHAEL KOGGE

SCHOLASTIC INC.

P9-BZJ-847

Copyright © 2018 Warner Bros. Entertainment Inc.

FANTASTIC BEASTS AND WHERE TO FIND THEM, FANTASTIC BEASTS: THE CRIMES OF GRINDELWALD,
HARRY POTTER characters, names, and related indicia are © & ™ Warner Bros. Entertainment Inc. WB SHIELD: TM & © WBEI.

WIZARDING WORLD trademark and logo © & ™ Warner Bros. Entertainment Inc. Publishing Rights © JKR. (s18)

www.harrypotter.com

www.fantasticbeasts.com

All rights reserved. Published by Scholastic Inc., *Publishers since 1920.* SCHOLASTIC and associated logos are trademarks
and/or registered trademarks of Scholastic Inc.

The publisher does not have any control over and does not assume any responsibility for author or third-party websites or their content.

No part of this publication may be reproduced, stored in a retrieval system, or transmitted in any form or by any means, electronic,
mechanical, photocopying, recording, or otherwise, without written permission of the publisher. For information regarding permission,
write to Scholastic Inc., Attention: Permissions Department, 557 Broadway, New York, NY 10012.

This book is a work of fiction. Names, characters, places, and incidents are either the product of the author's imagination or are used
fictitiously, and any resemblance to actual persons, living or dead, business establishments, events, or locales is entirely coincidental.

ISBN 978-1-338-32299-6

10 9 8 7 6 5 4 3 2 1   18 19 20 21 22

Photographs courtesy of Warner Bros. Entertainment Inc. Additional photos © 12-13 bricks: Nomad_Soul/Shutterstock;
14 bottom right coins: Sabelnikov/Shutterstock; 20-21 house silhouettes: astudio/Shutterstock and Natalie Rae/Shutterstock;
26-27 film strip: Tomislav Forgo/Shutterstock; 46 spiders: moj0j0/Shutterstock; 60 bottom right torn paper: Voin_Sveta/Shutterstock;
60, 61 claw marks: Chinch/Shutterstock; 60-61 background: Shebeko/Shutterstock; 76, 77 beige poster background:
Flat_Enot/Shutterstock.

Printed in the U.S.A. 40 • First printing 2018 • Additional illustrations by Betsy Peterschmidt
Designed by Betsy Peterschmidt & Erin McMahon

TABLE OF CONTENTS

WELCOME to the FILMS of the

LIVING SIDE BY SIDE

ordinary human society, hidden from sight, there are people who can call upon the wonders of magic. These witches and wizards can cast spells to transport themselves from one place to another, concoct potions of transformation, heal or hurt with a wave of a wand, and even ride broomsticks and beasts high among the clouds.

Witches and wizards exist across the globe in every country and continent, purposely keeping their communities and activities secret from non-magical society. As such, their existence in the larger world has remained secret, yet there is one way to experience the wizarding world: through the films of Harry Potter and Fantastic Beasts!

WIZARDING WORLD

But as we see in the films, magic alone does not diminish the capacity for conflict among people. Wizards can be as selfish and power hungry as the worst non-magical people.

Toward the beginning of the twentieth century and then near its end, practitioners of the Dark Arts have imperiled all that is good. If not for the courage and fortitude of a select few heroes during these eras, the great tides of darkness may have swallowed everything.

The names of two of these heroes are Newt Scamander and Harry Potter, and this is their world . . .

PART I:
MAGICAL
PLACES

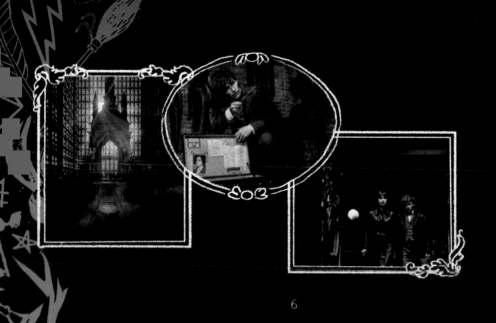

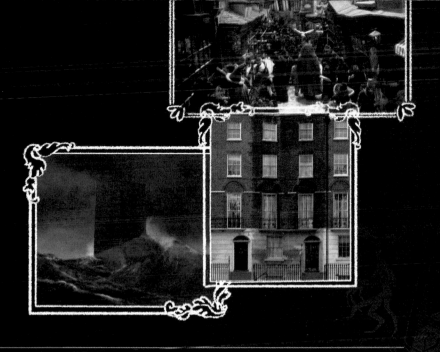

From the smallest wizarding pub to the grand castle of Hogwarts, the Wizarding World films abound with fantastical places. Fortunately, one doesn't need an Acceptance Letter from Hogwarts to explore its halls, or a handful of Floo Powder to observe the hustle and bustle of Diagon Alley. Read on to uncover the astonishing settings of Harry Potter and Fantastic Beasts!

GETTING AROUND:

PORTKEYS

Whenever they can, wizards and witches rely on either magical spells or the magic imbued in enchanted objects to travel from place to place.

PORTKEYS

are magical items that transport the one who holds or touches them to a designated place. Just about anything inanimate can be transformed into a Portkey, which are often everyday objects that won't attract a Muggle's attention, like old boots and buckets.

TURBULENT TRIPS: Using a Portkey can sometimes be rough on the landing, as Harry, Ron, and Hermione took a tumble using the leather boot Portkey in *Harry Potter and the Goblet of Fire!*

Unable to depart England by conventional means, Newt Scamander uses a **BUCKET** to transport both himself and Jacob Kowalski from the White Cliffs of Dover to Paris, France, in *Fantastic Beasts: The Crimes of Grindelwald.*

An **OLD LEATHER BOOT** takes Harry Potter and his friends from Stoatshead Hill to the Quidditch World Cup in *Harry Potter and the Goblet of Fire.*

Later in the same film, the **TRIWIZARD CUP** transports tournament co-champions Harry Potter and Cedric Diggory from Hogwarts to the Little Hangleton graveyard where Lord Voldemort waits.

Many of the fireplaces installed in the homes and buildings of the wizarding community are linked together in what is called the **FLOO NETWORK**. As we see in *Harry Potter and the Chamber of Secrets*, one need only announce the other fireplace within the network where they wish to go and sprinkle a handful of Floo Powder. Instantly, a bright green flame will appear—seemingly swallowing the user—and transport him or her unharmed to their final destination.

FLOO NETWORK

On a shopping trip for the new school year in *Harry Potter and the Chamber of Secrets*, Harry Potter and the Weasleys use **FLOO POWDER** to travel to Diagon Alley from the Weasleys' family home, known as The Burrow. Harry, unfortunately, mispronounces his destination and becomes momentarily lost Knockturn Alley.

MAGICAL WAYS TO TRAVEL

APPARITION

A difficult but very effective means of magical transportation is APPARITION. Wizards and witches who cast it, usually aided by a wand, can teleport themselves to a destination they've determined in their mind. If one isn't careful, Splinching can result, where part of a person is left behind at the original destination. This happened to Ron in *Harry Potter and the Deathly Hallows – Part 1*.

DOBBY the house-elf can Apparate at will, as he does throughout *Harry Potter and the Chamber of Secrets*. Dobby is killed by Bellatrix Lestrange while Disapparating out of Malfoy Manor in *Harry Potter and the Deathly Hallows – Part 1*.

Albus Dumbledore gives Harry Potter his first taste of Apparition while traveling to visit HORACE SLUGHORN before starting Harry's sixth year. Dumbledore compliments him, confiding, "Most people vomit the first time."

Newt Scamander grabs hold of NO-MAJ Jacob Kowalski and Apparates past the tellers and security guards in City Bank in *Fantastic Beasts and Where to Find Them*.

"I was—over there. I was—over *there*?"

Harry attempts to use the Floo Network again in *Harry Potter and the Order of the Phoenix* to transport himself, Ron, and Hermione to the Ministry of Magic via the FIREPLACE IN PROFESSOR UMBRIDGE'S OFFICE. Umbridge had all the other fireplaces at Hogwarts under close watch; unfortunately, Harry was intercepted before he could use it.

PERMISSION TO APPARATE: Certain places, such as the dungeon in Malfoy Manor, have Anti-Apparition spells placed on them that prevent people from Apparating in or Disapparating out of the space. Certain magical creatures, including house-elves, are not bound by Anti-Apparition spells.

BEAST TRANSPORT

When Apparating or using a Portkey is unsafe or not possible, wizards can travel with the help of magical creatures. Two creatures in particular, the THESTRAL and the HIPPOGRIFF, make excellent magical mounts.

HIPPOGRIFFS

The Hippogriff bears the beaked head, strong wings, and feathered front of a giant eagle, and the hindquarters and tail of a horse. In *Harry Potter and the Prisoner of Azkaban*, Harry mounts a Hippogriff named Buckbeak during his Care of Magical Creatures lesson. Hippogriffs are incredibly proud creatures—as Draco Malfoy learns, they are easily offended and will lash out if insulted.

HEROIC HIPPOGRIFF:

In their third year at Hogwarts, Harry and Hermione help Sirius Black evade capture on the back of Buckbeak.

THESTRALS

Thestrals are bony, horselike creatures with long necks, large bat-like wings, and a skeletal snout. Riding them can be a challenge, complicated by the fact they remain invisible to those who have never seen death.

ON A MISSION:

Harry and his friends ride Thestrals from the Forbidden Forest to the Ministry of Magic in *Harry Potter and the Order of the Phoenix*. Harry can see Thestrals because he had witnessed the death of Cedric Diggory during the previous school year.

PRISONER TRANSPORT: Thestrals pull the carriage containing MACUSA prisoner Gellert Grindelwald from America to Europe in *Fantastic Beasts: The Crimes of Grindelwald*.

MAGICAL VEHICLES

Icons of the wizarding community, BROOMSTICKS come in all different specifications and styles for wizards and witches to ride. Harry flew on both the Nimbus 2000 and Firebolt racing brooms during his Quidditch matches.

Hagrid delivers the baby Harry Potter to the Dursleys at number four, Privet Drive on his FLYING MOTORBIKE. In *Harry Potter and the Deathly Hallows – Part 1*, Hagrid fittingly takes Harry away from number four, Privet Drive for the last time on the same bike.

In *Harry Potter and the Goblet of Fire*, the DURMSTRANG SHIP transports the students of Durmstrang Institute to Hogwarts to participate in the Triwizard Tournament. The ship is shown magically submerging beneath the waves of Hogwarts' Black Lake.

Wizards needing a lift might hop on the triple-decker KNIGHT BUS, which zooms through busy streets and country roads and has beds for sleepy passengers. Harry is nearly run over by the bus before he jumps on, traveling from Little Whinging to the Leaky Cauldron in *Harry Potter and the Prisoner of Azkaban*.

The BEAUXBATONS CARRIAGE also travels to Hogwarts, but the carriage arrives by air, pulled by seven winged horses.

Painted sky blue, the Weasleys' FORD ANGLIA has been customized for flight, invisibility, and extra passengers, cargo, and pet space. The car is hardy, too, surviving a run-in with the Whomping Willow and an Acromantula attack in *Harry Potter and the Chamber of Secrets*.

VANISHING CABINETS open a magical passage that allows a person to enter one cabinet and come out the other. With Draco Malfoy's help, the Death Eaters use a Vanishing Cabinet in Borgin and Burkes antiques shop to enter Hogwarts undetected in *Harry Potter and the Half-Blood Prince*.

Hidden Entrances

Tapping a series of bricks in the wall behind the Leaky Cauldron pub opens DIAGON ALLEY for one's shopping delight.

To get onto PLATFORM NINE AND THREE-QUARTERS at King's Cross station and board the Hogwarts Express, one must run into the brick barrier between platforms nine and ten. Notably, Dobby the house-elf is able to close the entrance to Harry and Ron in *Harry Potter and the Chamber of Secrets*.

The Black family's London home at NUMBER TWELVE, GRIMMAULD PLACE is inaccessible to unwanted visitors. Only those who are aware of the home's existence can access it.

Visitors must dial a special number in the red telephone box outside Britain's MINISTRY OF MAGIC to be admitted into the Ministry's main building. An underground network of toilets in Whitehall also provides a means of entry into the Ministry's Atrium.

Wizards and witches hide the entrances to many magical places to keep them from non-wizards' eyes.

At the Woolworth Building in New York, one must approach the doorman for magical entry into the lobby of MAGICAL CONGRESS OF THE UNITED STATES OF AMERICA (MACUSA) HEADQUARTERS.

PLACE CACHÉE is a hidden street in 1920s Paris lined with magical shops. One can enter by walking through the concrete base of a statue.

One must walk into a Parisian fountain and descend via an elevator of tree roots to gain access to the MINISTÈRE DES AFFAIRES MAGIQUES DE LA FRANCE.

WIZARDING BANKS

As Harry learns in *Harry Potter and the Sorcerer's Stone*, Gringotts Wizarding Bank manages the money of Britain's wizarding community. Goblins work day and night to tally and supervise the deposits, withdrawals, monetary exchanges, and currency circulation.

LOCATION, LOCATION: The north side of Diagon Alley houses the central branch of Gringotts, making London the financial hub for wizards.

MAGIC MONEY: In Britain, the three denominations of wizarding coin are the gold Galleon, the silver Sickle, and the bronze Knut. One Galleon equates to 17 Sickles, while one Sickle is worth 29 Knuts. In the United States, most wizarding items are purchased using Dragots.

What's It Worth?

Pumpkin Pasty from the Hogwarts Express . . . . .1 Sickle

12-Month Subscription to the *New York Ghost* . . . . .5 Dragots

Weasleys' Wildfire Whiz-bangs . . . . .9 Sickles, 24 Knuts

Voges "The Elite" Self-Writing Quill . . . . .4.19 Dragots

Weasleys' Wizard Wheezes Magic Yo-Yo . . . . .5 Galleons
(10 Galleons for Ron)

Reward for Information Leading
to the Capture of Bellatrix Lestrange . . . . .1,000 Galleons

Reward for the Capture of Harry Potter
under Lord Voldemort's Ministry of Magic . . . . .10,000 Galleons

UNDER LOCK AND KEY: The underground vaults below the main branch of Gringotts are the most secure in the world. Wizarding families deposit their wealth here, protected by locks, charms, and even dragons. Valuable objects and artifacts are also guarded in these vaults, including the Sorcerer's Stone and one of Voldemort's Horcruxes, Helga Hufflepuff's Cup.

MAGICAL SHOPS

Throughout the Harry Potter and Fantastic Beasts films, characters often visit WIZARDING SHOPS to buy the magical objects they need.

IF YOU COULD VISIT ANY SHOP IN THE WIZARDING WORLD, WHAT WOULD YOU BE SHOPPING FOR?

A BIT OF FUN! BRITAIN OR FRANCE?

FRANCE

FUN OR FOOD?

FOOD

FUN

BRITAIN

LIGHT MISCHIEF OR DARK MISCHIEF?

DARK MISCHIEF

LIGHT MISCHIEF

SHOPPING FOR CLOTHES! ARE YOU AT SCHOOL?

YES

NO

HOGSMEADE: GLADRAGS WIZARDWEAR IS THE PERFECT PLACE TO PICK UP A NEW OUTFIT WHILE AT HOGWARTS.

BACK TO HOGWARTS SUPPLIES. ARE YOU A FIRST YEAR OR RETURNING STUDENT?

FIRST YEAR

DIAGON ALLEY: OLLIVANDERS CAN HELP YOU FIND THE WAND BEST SUITED TO YOU!

RETURNING

DIAGON ALLEY: PICK UP YOUR TEXTBOOKS AT FLOURISH AND BLOTTS!

KNOCKTURN ALLEY: BORGIN AND BURKES HAS ANTIQUES AND DARK RELICS OF ALL KINDS.

PLACE CACHÉE: CIRCUS ARCANUS FEATURES ODDITIES AND ACTS FROM EVERY CORNER OF THE WIZARDING WORLD.

LE CIRQUE ARCANUS
MUSÉE DES CURIOSITÉS VIVANTES

PLACE CACHÉE: THE DELECTABLE CONFISERIE MONSIEUR K. RAMMELLE CAN EQUIP YOU WITH ALL THE SWEETS YOU NEED TO GET YOU THROUGH THE YEAR.

DIAGON ALLEY: MADAM MALKIN'S ROBES FOR ALL OCCASIONS CAN TAILOR YOUR SCHOOL UNIFORM AND PROVIDE CASUAL AND DRESS ROBES.

HOGSMEADE: ZONKO'S JOKE SHOP HAS THE BEST PRANKS FOR THE HOGWARTS STUDENT ON THE GO!

ZONKO'S

DIAGON ALLEY: SCRIBBULUS WRITING IMPLEMENTS IS WELL-STOCKED WITH INKS, QUILLS, AND PARCHMENT.

DIAGON ALLEY: POTAGE'S CAULDRONS HAS EVERYTHING YOU NEED TO ACE POTIONS!

DIAGON ALLEY: WEASLEYS' WIZARD WHEEZES FEATURES PRODUCTS SUCH AS FAINTING FANCIES, EXTENDABLE EARS, AND AMORTENTIA—THE MOST POWERFUL LOVE POTION IN THE WORLD.

LOVE POTION

WIZARDING RESTAURANTS

Around the globe, there are special places that cater to a witch or wizard's appetite. Food and beverages are even tastier with a dash of magic!

THE THREE BROOMSTICKS

Madam Rosmerta's cozy pub in Hogsmeade is a favorite of Hogwarts students and faculty, who come mainly for the delicious Butterbeer. During *Harry Potter and the Prisoner of Azkaban*, Harry eavesdrops on a group of professors in the Three Broomsticks and learns that Sirius Black is his godfather.

THE HOG'S HEAD INN

Though also in Hogsmeade, the Hog's Head Inn doesn't offer much in the way of competition to the Three Broomsticks. It's dark and dingy inside, and its few patrons are usually of a disreputable character. Nonetheless, Hermione Granger thinks this makes the Hog's Head a perfect place for students to gather to discuss the formation of Dumbledore's Army in *Harry Potter and the Order of the Phoenix*.

THE LEAKY CAULDRON

Muggles walking on Charing Cross Road may think they're passing an abandoned storefront, but beyond this guise is one of the most boisterous wizarding pubs in the world. On his first trip to Diagon Alley, in *Harry Potter and the Sorcerer's Stone*, Harry Potter and Hagrid stay at the Leaky Cauldron.

KOWALSKI QUALITY BAKED GOODS

Though not magical, Jacob Kowalski starts this bakery in 1927, selling all sorts of strudels and Polish pastries, including ones shaped like magical creatures.

THE BLIND PIG

+ × + × ×

The goblin Gnarlak owns this little Manhattan speakeasy that requires a specific pattern of knocks to enter. A jazz singer croons wizarding tunes, and Gigglewater and Lobe Blaster are popular drinks. In 1926, Newt Scamander comes here to find out if Gnarlak has any information about his escaped beasts and Percival Graves.

CAFÉ ABRINGER

Tina meets the French-African wizard Yusuf Kama in this non-magic Parisian café.

HONEYDUKES

+ × + × ×

Though not quite a restaurant, this world-famous sweet shop in Hogsmeade is home to the most delectable confections in Britain.

THE BURROW: The Weasleys live in a towering, ramshackle house that came to be Harry's second home throughout the films.

LOVEGOOD HOUSE: Luna Lovegood grew up in this countryside tower that is later destroyed after her father tries to turn Harry, Ron, and Hermione over to Lord Voldemort in *Harry Potter and the Deathly Hallows – Part 1.*

NUMBER TWELVE, GRIMMAULD PLACE: Sirius Black's family once called this London townhouse home. It is filled with Dark magic relics, as well as a portrait of Walburga Black that insults Harry as he walks by it in *Harry Potter and the Order of the Phoenix.* The house is willed to Harry after Sirius's death.

SHELL COTTAGE: The eldest Weasley son, Bill, resides on the Cornwall coast in this charming beachside home with his wife, Fleur Delacour.

MALFOY MANOR: Voldemort's Death Eaters turn the estate home of the Malfoys into their base of operations in the Second Wizarding War. Many witches and wizards, including Harry himself, were held in the basement's dungeon.

MAGICAL HOMES

Just like everything else in the wizarding world, each WIZARDING HOME is unique and runs on all manners of magic.

GOLDSTEIN SISTERS' APARTMENT:
Tina and Queenie rent an apartment in Mrs. Esposito's New York brownstone.

NEWT'S LONDON FLAT:
When he's in London, Newt occupies an apartment between two London terraces. His basement is massive, allowing him the space to rehabilitate sick or injured creatures.

NICOLAS FLAMEL'S HOUSE:
The Paris home of Nicolas Flamel contains an intricate laboratory with all the vials, test tubes, and artifacts he's used over centuries of alchemy. A hidden vault in the wall contains the Sorcerer's Stone that Harry later encounters in *Harry Potter and the Sorcerer's Stone*.

NICOLAS FLAMEL
51 Rue de Montmorency
Paris

WIZARDING
SCHOOLS

HOGWARTS SCHOOL OF WITCHCRAFT AND WIZARDRY

LOCATION:
Scottish Highlands; serves students from all over the British Isles

UNIFORMS:
Students wear black robes and the colors of their designated houses.

NOTABLE ALUMNI:
Albus Dumbledore, Newt Scamander, Harry Potter

BEAUXBATONS ACADEMY OF MAGIC
(ACADÉMIE DE MAGIE BEAUXBÂTONS)

LOCATION:
The Pyrenees mountains in France; serves students from France and surrounding countries

UNIFORMS:
Students wear light blue silk robes.

NOTABLE ALUMNI:
Nicolas Flamel, Fleur Delacour

In Europe and North America, four main schools guide much of the education of young wizards and witches, who are usually inducted by age eleven. Britain's Ministry of Magic has laws in place that forbid students from performing magic outside of school.

Harry gets his first peek at other wizarding schools during *Harry Potter and the Goblet of Fire*, when Beauxbatons and Durmstrang visit Hogwarts to compete in the Triwizard Tournament.

In *Fantastic Beasts and Where to Find Them*, Queenie reveals to Jacob that Ilvermorny is the American wizarding school.

DURMSTRANG INSTITUTE

LOCATION:
Hidden somewhere in the far north of Europe; serves students from Northern Europe

UNIFORMS:
School uniforms are brown.

NOTABLE ALUMNI:
Gellert Grindelwald, Viktor Krum

ILVERMORNY SCHOOL OF WITCHCRAFT AND WIZARDRY

LOCATION:
Massachusetts in the United States; serves students from all over North America

UNIFORMS:
Like Hogwarts, students are divided into four houses; they wear blue and cranberry-red robes.

NOTABLE ALUMNI: Tina Goldstein, Queenie Goldstein, Seraphina Picquery

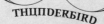
THUNDERBIRD

HOGWARTS

Founded at the turn of the first millennia, Hogwarts is renowned throughout the wizarding world as one of the premier institutions for the advanced education of magic.

QUIDDITCH: In the popular game of Quidditch, players ride broomsticks and attempt to throw a Quaffle ball through the opposing team's goal hoops. Hogwarts has its own field, called the Quidditch pitch, where students from each house compete to win the Quidditch Cup.

HOUSE CUP: Throughout their time at Hogwarts, students are awarded points based on good behavior and will lose points for rule-breaking. Points are tallied using enchanted hourglasses in the Great Hall, and at the end of the year, the house with the most points wins.

GROUNDS: The Hogwarts grounds have many unique features aside from the iconic castle, including the Black Lake and the Forbidden Forest. The grounds are also home to many wild magical creatures, as both Newt and Harry learn throughout their time there.

ADMISSION PROCESS: Any half-blood, pure-blood, or Muggle-born children demonstrating magical abilities are enrolled at Hogwarts.

BIRTHDAY PRESENT: When a witch or wizard nears the age of eleven, the Owl Post delivers an Acceptance Letter like the one Harry Potter received in *Harry Potter and the Sorcerer's Stone*.

GRYFFINDOR

GHOST: SIR NICHOLAS (NEARLY HEADLESS NICK)

FOUNDER: GODRIC GRYFFINDOR

COLORS: SCARLET & GOLD

ANIMAL: LION

ARTIFACT: SWORD OF GRYFFINDOR

MEMBER QUALITIES: COURAGE, BRAVERY, DETERMINATION

NOTABLE MEMBERS: HARRY POTTER, HERMIONE GRANGER, WEASLEY FAMILY, NEVILLE LONGBOTTOM

SLYTHERIN

FOUNDER: SALAZAR SLYTHERIN

ANIMAL: SERPENT

COLORS: GREEN & SILVER

MEMBER QUALITIES: PROUD, AMBITIOUS, CUNNING

GHOST: THE BLOODY BARON

ARTIFACT: SALAZAR SLYTHERIN'S LOCKET

NOTABLE MEMBERS: TOM RIDDLE (LORD VOLDEMORT), SEVERUS SNAPE, MALFOY FAMILY

HOUSES

The Sorting Hat places students into their academic houses based on their individual values and traits. Students will stay with their other house members in house dormitories and share the house Common Room.

RAVENCLAW

ANIMAL: RAVEN

FOUNDER: ROWENA RAVENCLAW

COLORS: BLUE & SILVER

GHOST: HELENA RAVENCLAW (THE GRAY LADY)

MEMBER QUALITIES: WIT, INTELLIGENCE, WISDOM

ARTIFACT: ROWENA RAVENCLAW'S DIADEM

NOTABLE MEMBERS: LUNA LOVEGOOD, CHO CHANG, GILDEROY LOCKHART

HUFFLEPUFF

FOUNDER: HELGA HUFFLEPUFF

ANIMAL: BADGER

COLORS: YELLOW & BLACK

ARTIFACT: HELGA HUFFLEPUFF'S CUP

GHOST: THE FAT FRIAR

MEMBER QUALITIES: PATIENCE, LOYALTY, FAIR-MINDED

NOTABLE MEMBERS: NEWT SCAMANDER, NYMPHADORA TONKS, CEDRIC DIGGORY

HOGWARTS STUDENT LIFE

As young students, Leta Lestrange forges a deep connection with Newt Scamander after she finds him caring for a raven chick.

According to his MACUSA file, Newt put the life of another student at risk during an incident with a magical creature. Despite Professor Dumbledore's support, Newt is expelled from Hogwarts.

THEN & NOW

James Potter, Sirius Black, Remus Lupin, and Peter Pettigrew become friends at Hogwarts. The four draw up a detailed layout of Hogwarts' grounds known as the Marauder's Map. James Potter befriends a female student, Lily Evans, whom he will later marry.

Harry Potter enrolls in Hogwarts, befriends Hermione Granger and Ron Weasley, and overcomes a great number of challenges, from beating the Basilisk in the Chamber of Secrets to overthrowing Dolores Umbridge and restoring Dumbledore to the headmaster position in *Harry Potter and the Order of the Phoenix*. But his biggest challenge proves to be outwitting Tom Riddle, now known as Lord Voldemort, and surviving the Dark Lord's many attempts on his life.

Headmaster Albus Dumbledore is slain atop the Astronomy Tower and laid to rest on the Hogwarts grounds in the White Tomb in *Harry Potter and the Half-Blood Prince*.

Torquil Travers, the head of the Ministry of Magic's law enforcement division, interrupts Professor Dumbledore's class and interrogates him about his former pupil, Newt Scamander. Travers removes Dumbledore from teaching Defense Against the Dark Arts.

The Muggle world undergoes tremendous change during the twentieth century, as does Hogwarts, which is front and center in many major magical conflicts.

In flashbacks from *Harry Potter and the Chamber of Secrets*, Tom Marvolo Riddle, a fifth-year Slytherin student, opens the Chamber of Secrets. The Chamber holds a Basilisk, which kills a female student named Myrtle Warren. The Ministry of Magic threatens to close the school. Riddle makes it seem like the half-giant Hagrid is to blame for Myrtle's death, and that the act was committed by an Acromantula, not a Basilisk. Hagrid is expelled, his wand taken; Tom evades punishment.

Harry Potter leads his fellow students in the Battle of Hogwarts against the Dark Lord's forces and destroys Lord Voldemort once and for all. During the battle, Hogwarts itself suffers great damage.

Harry, Ginny, Hermione, and Ron take their children to King's Cross station for the new school year at Hogwarts.

HOGWARTS CLASSES

Students at Hogwarts follow a standardized path of coursework, with the ability to choose additional courses depending on availability and interest.

ASTRONOMY

Students observe and study the stars and planetary movements.

HERBOLOGY

Knowledge about plants and fungi can assist students in gathering ingredients for potions or using the magical properties of the natural world.

CHARMS

Students learn spells that alter what an object does, such as levitating an object or amplifying one's voice.

TRANSFIGURATION

One of the most difficult courses. As opposed to charms, transfigurations actually alter the appearance and form of things. Transfiguration spells can turn an animal into a water goblet, or a person into a ferret.

POTIONS

Methods of recognizing potions, brewing potions, and gathering potion ingredients are taught in this class, though Harry gets some extra help from his annotated textbook in *Harry Potter and the Half-Blood Prince*.

History of Magic

As the name implies, students are lectured on events and persons that shaped the magical world.

Defense Against the Dark Arts

This course instructs students on methods to protect themselves against dangerous Dark creatures, relics, and spells.

Flying Lessons

Harry, Ron, and Hermione must master flying a broomstick in *Harry Potter and the Sorcerer's Stone.*

Third-year students may pick two or more electives to add to their course load such as:

Care of Magical Creatures

This introductory course in Magizoology teaches students the properties of various fantastic beasts and the basics of maintaining them.

Divination

Harry and Ron take this class in *Harry Potter and the Prisoner of Azkaban*, where they learn rituals and use certain tools to discern how to glimpse the future and obtain insight and foreknowledge.

Muggle Studies

This subject provides wizards and witches with a broad examination of Muggle culture and how Muggles live.

Ancient Runes

Students learn how to read and translate the runes written ages ago by ancient wizards and witches.

HOGWARTS HEADMASTERS AND PROFESSORS

PROFESSORS

HORACE SLUGHORN
Professor of Potions

RUBEUS HAGRID
Professor of Care of
Magical Creatures

ROLANDA HOOCH
Flying Instructor

MINERVA McGONAGALL
Professor of Transfiguration

POMONA SPROUT
Professor of Herbology

CHARITY BURBAGE
Professor of
Muggle Studies

ALECTO CARROW
Professor of
Muggle Studies

FILIUS FLITWICK
Professor of Charms

SYBILL TRELAWNEY
Professor of Divination

DEFENSE AGAINST THE DARK ARTS PROFESSORS

It was said that the DEFENSE AGAINST THE DARK ARTS POST was jinxed so that no one could hold the job for more than a year. This proves true throughout Harry's time at Hogwarts.

QUIRINUS QUIRRELL
(Perished in
pursuit of the
Sorcerer's Stone)

GILDEROY LOCKHART
(Suffered spell damage
caused by a backfired
Memory Charm)

REMUS LUPIN
(Resigned after it was
discovered he was a
werewolf)

BARTEMIUS CROUCH JR.
posing as Alastor "Mad-Eye" Moody
(Arrested after the Triwizard
Tournament)

DOLORES UMBRIDGE
(Driven out by centaurs)

SEVERUS SNAPE
(Previously professor of
Potions, later promoted
to headmaster)

AMYCUS CARROW
(Arrested after the
Battle of Hogwarts)

HEADMASTERS

Hogwarts has never lacked in colorful HEADMASTERS and PROFESSORS during the last century.

ALBUS DUMBLEDORE

DOLORES UMBRIDGE

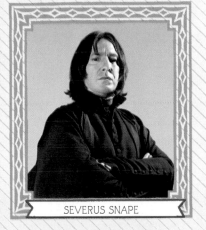

SEVERUS SNAPE

MINERVA McGONAGALL

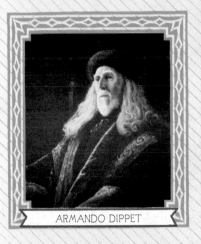

ARMANDO DIPPET

EVERARD

USEFUL PORTRAITS: Everard and Phineas have portraits in other locations besides the headmaster's office at Hogwarts. Everard's portrait also hangs in the Ministry of Magic, while Phineas has another portrait at number twelve, Grimmauld Place. This makes it easy for the Headmaster of Hogwarts to communicate with either the Ministry or the Order of the Phoenix at a moment's notice, as seen in *Harry Potter and the Order of the Phoenix.*

PHINEAS NIGELLUS BLACK

Wizarding Governments

Wizarding communities usually establish their own governments in their countries of residence, yet most share a set of common laws.

British Ministry of Magic

MINISTRY OF MAGIC

THE MINISTRY OF MAGIC upholds and enforces wizarding laws all over the United Kingdom.

LOCATION: The Ministry of Magic is situated in Whitehall, London, which is also the center of Britain's Muggle government. The Ministry offices are deep underground and therefore out of sight of Muggles.

NOTABLE OFFICIALS

1900

1927

Theseus Scamander, Head of the British Auror Office (1927)

Hector Fawley, Minister for Magic (1927)

Torquil Travers, Head of Magical Law Enforcement (1927)

INTERNATIONAL CONFEDERATION OF WIZARDS: Representatives from wizarding governments around the world meet and discuss resolutions to global problems.

INTERNATIONAL STATUTE OF SECRECY: In 1692, after the persecution of wizards and witches by non-magical beings in Europe and North America, the International Confederation passes the International Statute of Secrecy. It requires wizards and witches to conceal their use of magic and keep the wizarding world secret from non-magical beings. Those who break the law face grave punishment, something Harry confronts for the first time when he and Ron drive the Weasleys' Ford Anglia over London in *Harry Potter and the Chamber of Secrets*.

INSIDE THE MINISTRY

HEARING ROOM: In *Fantastic Beasts: The Crimes of Grindelwald*, Newt Scamander faces a panel of officials led by Torquil Travers regarding his request for permission to return to the United States. He is banned from international travel for refusing to help them capture the Obscurus.

COURTROOM TEN: The Ministry convenes major hearings of the Wizengamot here, such as the one against Harry Potter for casting a Patronus Charm outside of school before his fifth year at Hogwarts. Harry is acquitted after Dumbledore comes to his defense.

DEPARTMENT OF MYSTERIES: This restricted area houses prophecies, artifacts, and unique phenomena that are being further explored by Ministry officials. It is here that Harry and Dumbledore's Army do battle with the Death Eaters in *Harry Potter and the Order of the Phoenix*.

WIZENGAMOT: Representatives from the British wizarding community meet to pass laws as well as judgments for serious crimes. Dumbledore, Dolores Umbridge, and Amelia Bones (the aunt of Harry's classmate, Susan Bones) all have held positions on the Wizengamot. A Chief Warlock presides over the chamber. Past Chief Warlocks include Barty Crouch Sr. and Cornelius Fudge, who presides over Harry's trial in *Harry Potter and the Order of the Phoenix*.

Cornelius Fudge, Minister for Magic (1990-1996) — 1992

Rufus Scrimgeour, Minister for Magic (1996-1997)

Kingsley Shacklebolt named Acting Minister for Magic (1998); later assumed official position — 1997

2000

1990 — Arthur Weasley, Head of the Misuse of Muggle Artifacts Office (1992) — 1996

Pius Thicknesse, Minister for Magic, under Imperious Curse (1996-1997)

1998

MACUSA

LOCATION: MACUSA houses its headquarters in the Woolworth Building at 233 Broadway in New York City.

THE MAGICAL CONGRESS OF THE UNITED STATES OF AMERICA, also known as MACUSA, oversees the wizarding community in the United States.

Ministère des Affaires Magiques de la France

LOCATION: Under the streets of Paris, nestled between its sewers and crypts, are the chambers and passages of the Ministère des Affaires Magiques de la France.

MINISTÈRE DES AFFAIRES MAGIQUES DE LA FRANCE governs the wizards and witches across France.

INSIDE MACUSA

Wand Permit Office: To use a wand in the United States in 1927, wizards and witches need to be licensed.

Lobby: A Magical Exposure Threat Level Clock predicts how close the wizarding community is to being revealed to the No-Maj world.

Pentagram Office: In this chamber, Newt Scamander is questioned by the International Confederation of Wizards about the magical disturbances in New York in *Fantastic Beasts and Where to Find Them*.

Prison Cells: MACUSA jails wizards who break their laws. At different times, this included both Newt Scamander and Gellert Grindelwald.

NOTABLE OFFICIALS

In 1926, SERAPHINA PICQUERY serves as MACUSA's president. Her challenge is to continue to keep the No-Majs ignorant of the magical world and avert a potential war. This becomes more difficult with the New Salem Philanthropic Society's crusade against witchcraft and the accidental release of Newt Scamander's beasts into New York's streets.

Foyer: This vast underground room has a domed ceiling emblazoned with a wizarding astrological chart.

Vault: The Ministère's immense library keeps records in row after row of towers.

Ministère des Affaires Magiques de la France: The Ministère's chambers are accessed by the roots of a tree, which form a cage around entrants and lower them beneath the ground.

AZKABAN

FAMOUS INMATES AND THEIR CRIMES

WANTED
BY THE MINISTRY OF MAGIC

BELLATRIX LESTRANGE

BELLATRIX LESTRANGE IS A KNOWN DEATH EATER,
CONVICTED MURDERER, FUGITIVE FROM AZKABAN.

★ APPROACH WITH EXTREME CAUTION! ★

IF YOU HAVE ANY INFORMATION CONCERNING
THIS PERSON, PLEASE CONTACT YOUR
NEAREST AUROR OFFICE.

☞ **REWARD** ☜

THE MINISTRY OF MAGIC IS OFFERING A REWARD OF 1,000 GALLEONS
FOR INFORMATION LEADING DIRECTLY TO THE ARREST OF BELLATRIX LESTRANGE.

BELLATRIX LESTRANGE was a known Death Eater and convicted murderer. She used the Cruciatus Curse on Neville Longbottom's parents, torturing them to insanity.

FENRIR GREYBACK was a suspected Death Eater and convicted murderer. He turned multiple people into werewolves, including Remus Lupin. Bill Weasley survived an attack by Greyback; although he didn't become a werewolf, he bears a scar from the incident.

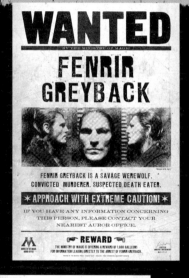

WANTED
BY THE MINISTRY OF MAGIC

FENRIR GREYBACK

FENRIR GREYBACK IS A SAVAGE WEREWOLF,
CONVICTED MURDERER, SUSPECTED DEATH EATER.

★ APPROACH WITH EXTREME CAUTION! ★

IF YOU HAVE ANY INFORMATION CONCERNING
THIS PERSON, PLEASE CONTACT YOUR
NEAREST AUROR OFFICE.

☞ **REWARD** ☜

THE MINISTRY OF MAGIC IS OFFERING A REWARD OF 1,000 GALLEONS
FOR INFORMATION LEADING DIRECTLY TO THE ARREST OF FENRIR GREYBACK.

CAUGHT
BY THE MINISTRY OF MAGIC

LUCIUS MALFOY

CONSTANT VIGILANCE!

DEATH EATERS ARE AMONG US!

★ REMEMBER: NEGLIGENCE COSTS LIVES ★

IF YOU HAVE ANY INFORMATION CONCERNING
DEATH EATERS, PLEASE CONTACT YOUR
NEAREST AUROR OFFICE.

☞ **REWARD** ☜

THE MINISTRY OF MAGIC IS OFFERING A REWARD OF 1,000 GALLEONS
FOR INFORMATION LEADING DIRECTLY TO THE ARREST OF ANY DEATH EATER.

LUCIUS MALFOY was convicted of being a Death Eater following the battle at the Department of Mysteries in *Harry Potter and the Order of the Phoenix.*

AMYCUS CARROW and ALECTO CARROW were both known associates and suspected Death Eaters of Lord Voldemort.

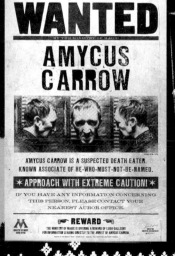

WANTED
BY THE MINISTRY OF MAGIC

AMYCUS CARROW

AMYCUS CARROW IS A SUSPECTED DEATH EATER,
KNOWN ASSOCIATE OF HE-WHO-MUST-NOT-BE-NAMED.

★ APPROACH WITH EXTREME CAUTION! ★

IF YOU HAVE ANY INFORMATION CONCERNING
THIS PERSON, PLEASE CONTACT YOUR
NEAREST AUROR OFFICE.

☞ **REWARD** ☜

THE MINISTRY OF MAGIC IS OFFERING A REWARD OF 1,000 GALLEONS
FOR INFORMATION LEADING DIRECTLY TO THE ARREST OF AMYCUS CARROW.

The fortress of AZKABAN, built on a lonely island in the rough waters of the North Sea, imprisons the most dangerous criminals in the wizarding world. During Harry's time at Hogwarts, Azkaban was guarded by Dementors.

HAVE YOU SEEN THIS WIZARD?

AZKABAN PRISON
1390

APPROACH WITH EXTREME CAUTION!
DO NOT ATTEMPT TO USE
MAGIC AGAINST THIS MAN!

Any information leading to the arrest of this
man shall be duly rewarded

Notify immediately by owl the Ministry of Magic

RUBEUS HAGRID was falsely accused of opening the Chamber of Secrets for the second time during *Harry Potter and the Chamber of Secrets*. It was later discovered that Voldemort had opened the Chamber by controlling Ginny Weasley through Dark magic.

WANTED
BY THE MINISTRY OF MAGIC

★ APPROACH WITH EXTREME CAUTION! ★

IF YOU HAVE ANY INFORMATION CONCERNING
THIS PERSON, PLEASE CONTACT YOUR
NEAREST AUROR OFFICE.

☞ REWARD ☜
THE MINISTRY OF MAGIC IS OFFERING A REWARD OF 1,000 GALLEONS
FOR INFORMATION LEADING DIRECTLY TO THE ARREST OF BELLATRIX LESTRANGE

SIRIUS BLACK was falsely accused of murdering twelve Muggles and Peter Pettigrew. Unbeknownst to the Ministry, Peter had transformed himself into a rat, forcing Sirius to be blamed for his crimes as well as for the deaths of James and Lily Potter.

REPEAT OFFENDER

GELLERT GRINDELWALD was wanted for many crimes throughout his early life. As a young man, he stole the Elder Wand from the wandmaker Gregorovitch, and he rose to power during Newt's time, committing many horrible crimes. In *Harry Potter and the Deathly Hallows – Part 1*, Lord Voldemort visited him in another prison, Nurmengard, seeking information about the Elder Wand.

Magical Breakouts AND Break-Ins

Some magical places have been deemed impenetrable and inescapable—until a determined witch, wizard, or group proves them wrong.

THE NEW YORK GHOST

DANGEROUS CRIMINALS AT LARGE!

Magizoologist Newt Scamander and former Auror Tina Goldstein escape from the MACUSA Death Chamber in *Fantastic Beasts and Where to Find Them* with the help of Pickett the Bowtruckle and a Swooping Evil. Percival Graves had sentenced them to death for breaking the International Statute of Secrecy and causing mass disruption in New York.

GRINDELWALD ESCAPES!

Gellert Grindelwald wrests free of his bonds and takes control of the carriage that is bringing him back to Europe to face punishment for his crimes prior to *Fantastic Beasts and Where to Find Them*. In the mêlée, Grindelwald recaptures his wand and blasts his guard, Rudolph Spielman, out the carriage window.

witch beguile · spellbind conjure enchant divinate

The DAILY PROPHET

✶ THE WIZARD WORLD'S BEGUILING BROADSHEET OF CHOICE ✶

THE DAILY PROPHET COMPETITION
WIN A WEEKEND FOR 2
BEST CLIMBING IN THE RELAXING
SURROUNDING OF ROMANIA.
FULL REPORT PAGE 465

National Weather
south - sunny period 3c
north - cloudy & rain 7c
central - cloudy & rain 3c
London - sunny period 5c

Zodiac ✶ Aspects

First/Second Edition
Nº 982745 - London - UK
Monday ☾ in Scorpio
Letters to the Editor should be sent "by owl" to
the Daily Prophet, Diagon Alley, London

MASS BREAKOUT
FROM AZKABAN

In *Harry Potter and the Order of the Phoenix*, convicts Bellatrix Lestrange, Augustus Rookwood, and Antonin Dolohov lead seven other Death Eaters in a wild escape from the desolate island prison. They persuade their Dementor guards to join their side and assist them in their release. Minister for Magic Cornelius Fudge mistakenly believes Sirius Black directed the jailbreak (Sirius had escaped prison, unaided, two years earlier).

HARRY POTTER
BREAKS INTO
GRINGOTTS

Using Polyjuice Potion, Transfiguration, and the Cloak of Invisibility, Harry, Ron, Hermione, and the goblin Griphook, a former employee of Gringotts, break into Bellatrix Lestrange's vault at Gringotts and steal Helga Hufflepuff's cup. They escape on the back of a guard dragon that bursts through the roof of the bank in *Harry Potter and the Deathly Hallows – Part 2*.

SUMMER BREAK [OUT]!

Fred, George, and Ron Weasley bust Harry out of number four, Privet Drive in *Harry Potter and the Chamber of Secrets* by stealing their father's flying Ford Anglia and pulling the bars off Harry's windows.

PART II:
MAGICAL
PEOPLE

The Wizarding World is nothing without the many people who inhabit it. From Muggle-born witches and wizards new to the delights of magic to the most ancient and noble wizarding families steeped in the ways of the magical world, it is people who determine the course of history. Though it is often a result of peoples' differing visions for the Wizarding World that immerse that same world in conflict.

HARRY POTTER

"EVERY GREAT WIZARD IN HISTORY HAS STARTED OUT AS NOTHING MORE THAN WHAT WE ARE NOW, STUDENTS. IF THEY CAN DO IT, WHY NOT US?"
- Harry Potter speaking to Dumbledore's Army

AS A BABY, HARRY POTTER

survives Lord Voldemort's Killing Curse, protected by the love and sacrifice of his mother. This act marks him as the Chosen One, destined to someday defeat the Dark Lord. After the death of his parents, Harry grows up in the care of his Muggle aunt and uncle, who treat their orphaned nephew as a second-class citizen next to their own son. But when Harry is eleven, he is accepted at Hogwarts School of Witchcraft and Wizardry. For the next six years, Harry Potter meets many new friends and learns how to use his innate talents, discovering the truth about his connection to Lord Voldemort along the way. At the age of seventeen, he rallies a resistance army of witches and wizards and defeats the Dark Lord once and for all.

Full Name: HARRY JAMES POTTER

Family: PARENTS, JAMES POTTER AND LILY POTTER (NÉE EVANS)

Schooling: HOGWARTS, GRYFFINDOR HOUSE

LORD VOLDEMORT

"You're a fool, Harry Potter. And you will lose everything!"
— Lord Voldemort

LORD VOLDEMORT BEGINS

his life as Tom Riddle, abandoned by his father and raised in a London orphanage, after his mother–a descendant of Salazar Slytherin–dies after childbirth. At Hogwarts, Tom finds the home he always longed for, becoming a powerful wizard and delving deeply into the Dark Arts. After graduating, Tom splits his soul into seven Horcruxes and declares himself Lord Voldemort, mustering an army of creatures and wizards to do his dark bidding. Only the boy Harry Potter stands in the way of his total domination of the wizarding world.

Full Name: TOM MARVOLO RIDDLE

Family: PARENTS, TOM RIDDLE, MEROPE RIDDLE (NÉE GAUNT)

Schooling: HOGWARTS, SLYTHERIN HOUSE

NEWT SCAMANDER

"THERE ARE NO STRANGE CREATURES—ONLY BLINKERED PEOPLE."
—Newt Scamander to Leta Lestrange

FROM AN EARLY AGE,

Newt Scamander knows he has an affinity for magical creatures and spends much of his time at Hogwarts studying them before his expulsion. He later joins the Beast Division of the Ministry of Magic, and during the Great War works with Ukrainian Ironbelly dragons on the Eastern Front. After the war, a publisher commissions Newt to pen a book about fantastic beasts, and so begins Newt's adventures around the world in search of magical creatures. But when Albus Dumbledore insists he cannot act against Gellert Grindelwald, Newt gets caught up in a larger conflict among wizardkind.

Full Name: NEWTON ("NEWT") ARTEMIS FIDO SCAMANDER

Family: BROTHER, THESEUS SCAMANDER

Schooling: HOGWARTS, HUFFLEPUFF HOUSE

GELLERT GRINDELWALD

"WILL WE DIE JUST A LITTLE?"
—Gellert Grindelwald to Newt Scamander

THE DURMSTRANG INSTITUTE

has a reputation for instructing students in the Dark Arts, but Gellert Grindelwald develops a passion for the subject. Expelled from Durmstrang, Grindelwald befriends Albus Dumbledore and persuades the young wizard to share in his vision to end the International Statute of Secrecy. The two become close allies until an unknown conflict leads them to become estranged. Grindelwald turns his sights toward sparking a global revolution among wizards. He believes wizards and witches should not hide themselves from the non-wizards, but make themselves leaders of a better world. For some time, Grindelwald wanders New York in the guise of the wizard Percival Graves, searching for the Obscurial whom he can use as a weapon to achieve his ends. Though captured, he escapes from custody and continues his work in Paris, gathering followers.

Full Name: GELLERT GRINDELWALD

Parents: UNKNOWN

Schooling: DURMSTRANG INSTITUTE

FRIENDS INDEED

Neither Newt Scamander nor Harry Potter can survive or succeed in their quests by themselves. Along the way, they make lifelong magical friends who remain loyal through thick and thin.

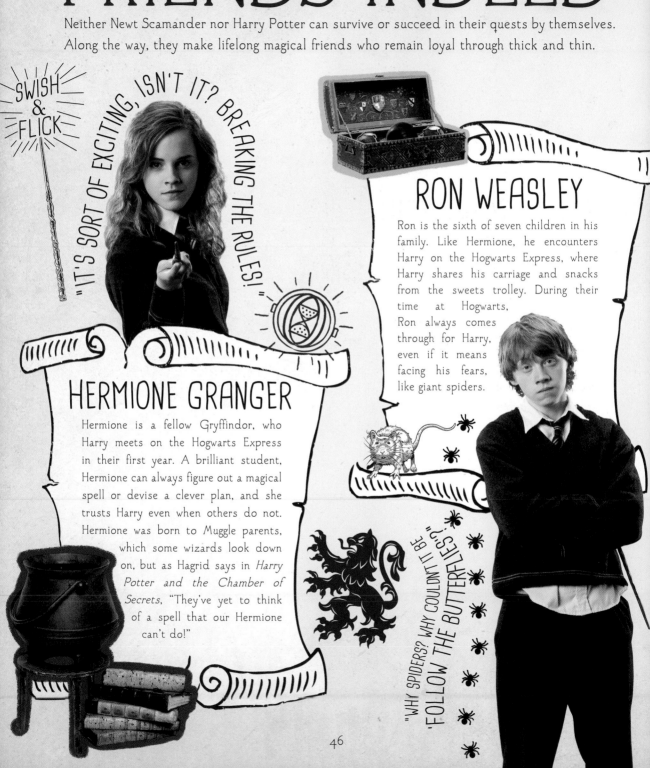

SWISH & FLICK

"IT'S SORT OF EXCITING, ISN'T IT? BREAKING THE RULES!"

HERMIONE GRANGER

Hermione is a fellow Gryffindor, who Harry meets on the Hogwarts Express in their first year. A brilliant student, Hermione can always figure out a magical spell or devise a clever plan, and she trusts Harry even when others do not. Hermione was born to Muggle parents, which some wizards look down on, but as Hagrid says in *Harry Potter and the Chamber of Secrets*, "They've yet to think of a spell that our Hermione can't do!"

RON WEASLEY

Ron is the sixth of seven children in his family. Like Hermione, he encounters Harry on the Hogwarts Express, where Harry shares his carriage and snacks from the sweets trolley. During their time at Hogwarts, Ron always comes through for Harry, even if it means facing his fears, like giant spiders.

"WHY SPIDERS? WHY COULDN'T IT BE 'FOLLOW THE BUTTERFLIES'?"

QUEENIE GOLDSTEIN

A gregarious extrovert, Queenie is the opposite of her quiet, often more serious sister. Her magical talents lend themselves to creative pursuits, like mending dresses and Legilimency, the ability to read others' minds. Her extraordinary gifts come in handy when she needs to rescue Newt, Jacob Kowalski, and her sister from Obliviators and executioners in MACUSA.

TINA GOLDSTEIN

Porpentina "Tina" and Queenie Goldstein lost their parents to dragon pox at an early age. A keen observer, Tina graduates from Ilvermorny and joins the ranks of the MACUSA Aurors. But her relentless obsession with a single case gets her demoted to Wand Permit Officer. She catches Newt breaking the International Statute of Secrecy and brings him in for questioning, though eventually she sides with him and helps expose Grindelwald. Tina and Newt have a complicated relationship–neither can admit their feelings for the other–a situation that only gets more complicated when Tina travels to Paris in *Fantastic Beasts: The Crimes of Grindelwald*.

ALL WAND ID **INFORMATION** WILL BE KEPT **CONFIDENTIAL**

BUNTY

Newt's dedicated assistant shares his love of fantastic beasts and watches over his London menagerie while he's away. Bunty is eager to learn as much as she can from Newt and shares his vision for educating people about the need to protect magical creatures.

ORDER OF THE PHOENIX

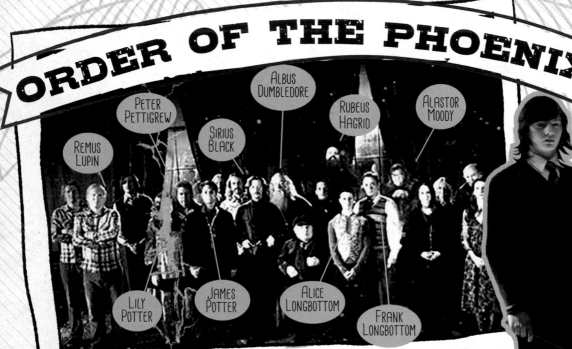

Remus Lupin · Peter Pettigrew · Sirius Black · Albus Dumbledore · Rubeus Hagrid · Alastor Moody · Lily Potter · James Potter · Alice Longbottom · Frank Longbottom

Dumbledore establishes this covert group of wizards and witches to counter Lord Voldemort's Death Eaters during the First Wizarding War. The Order disbands after the defeat of Lord Voldemort, but reassembles fourteen years later when the Dark Lord returns.

FULL NAME: Albus Percival Wulfric Brian Dumbledore
PARENTS: Percival and Kendra Dumbledore
SCHOOLING: Hogwarts, Gryffindor House

Albus Dumbledore met tragedy at a young age after the loss of his parents and sister, Ariana. As a young man, he met Gellert Grindelwald, who was visiting his aunt, the celebrated historian Bathilda Bagshot.

ALBUS DUMBLEDORE

DUMBLEDORE'S ARMY

When the Ministry of Magic interferes in educating students about Defense Against the Dark Arts in *Harry Potter and the Order of the Phoenix*, Hermione starts a secret resistance organization known as Dumbledore's Army, where Harry teaches offensive and defensive magic. After Harry, Ron, and Hermione leave school to hunt Horcruxes, the students, led by Neville Longbottom, Ginny Weasley, and Seamus Finnigan, continue the resistance against Lord Voldemort.

FRED WEASLEY · PADMA PATIL · GEORGE WEASLEY · NEVILLE LONGBOTTOM · DEAN THOMAS · PARVATI PATIL · CHO CHANG · HARRY POTTER · HERMIONE GRANGER · RON WEASLEY · LUNA LOVEGOOD · GINNY WEASLEY

"HAPPINESS CAN BE FOUND EVEN IN THE DARKEST OF TIMES, IF ONE ONLY REMEMBERS TO TURN ON THE LIGHT."

–Albus Dumbledore

The two became fast and close friends, but grew apart for unknown reasons. Dumbledore then set his sights on becoming a professor at Hogwarts, where he works for the rest of his life. Over his many decades at Hogwarts, he rises to the distinguished position of headmaster and helps lead the fight against both Grindelwald and, later, Lord Voldemort.

PRACTITIONERS

GRINDELWALD'S ACOLYTES:
Grindelwald's attacks across the world don't stop other wizards and witches from flocking to his cause. These followers–his acolytes–break international wizarding laws and ethical codes in pursuit of Grindelwald's agenda: to bring the wizarding world out of hiding and take the world for themselves.

VINDA ROSIER

NOTABLE MEMBERS

ABERNATHY

OTHER MEMBERS

Carrow

Krafft

Krall

Nagel

Macduff

OF THE DARK ARTS

LORD VOLDEMORT'S DEATH EATERS:

Like Grindelwald, Lord Voldemort has his own supporters, a group of witches and wizards well-versed in the Dark Arts. The Death Eaters believe that magical pure-bloods should reign supreme, with the Dark Lord above all. Many hide their faces behind hoods and grotesque masks, and are branded with the Dark Mark.

NOTABLE MEMBERS

BELLATRIX LESTRANGE

LUCIUS MALFOY

DRACO MALFOY

SEVERUS SNAPE
(LATER A DOUBLE AGENT FOR THE ORDER OF THE PHOENIX)

OTHER MEMBERS

ALECTO AND AMYCUS CARROW

BARTY CROUCH JR.

ANTONIN DOLOHOV

RODOLPHUS LESTRANGE

WALDEN MACNAIR

PETER PETTIGREW

AUGUSTUS ROOKWOOD

TRAVERS

CORBAN YAXLEY

WEASLEY FAMILY TREE

Arthur
Weasley

Molly Weasley
(née Prewett)

Bill Weasley

Fleur Weasley
(née Delacour)

Charlie Weasley

Percy Weasley

Fred Weasley

George Weasley

Ronald Weasley

Hermione Granger

Hugo Granger-Weasley

Rose Granger-Weasley

Ginny Potter
(née Weasley)

Harry Potter

James Potter

Albus Potter

Lily Potter

BROTHERS: Ron and Percy Weasley's relationship somewhat mirrors that of Newt and Theseus Scamander. Percy and Theseus are both by-the-book overachievers who seek to follow the letter of the law. Ron and Newt are more free-spirited and are willing to overstep traditional boundaries to do what they believe is right.

Though less common in Harry's time, a witch or wizard's "blood status" sadly defines their position in many wizarding communities and families.

PURE-BLOODS are those with parents of entirely magical ancestry. Many pure-bloods consider themselves superior to everyone else, though some, like the Weasleys, are more progressive.

HALF-BLOODS possess one parent who is a pure-blood and the other who is a Muggle or Muggle-born.

MUGGLE-BORNS are born from ordinary Muggle parents, but inherit the trait to perform magic from an often unknown ancestor. Some wizards, like Draco Malfoy, use the insulting term "Mudblood" to refer to people with this status.

THE NOBLE AND MOST ANCIENT HOUSE OF BLACK

The House of Black has always been proud of their pure-blood status, and most in the family, aside from Sirius, have used it to their advantage.

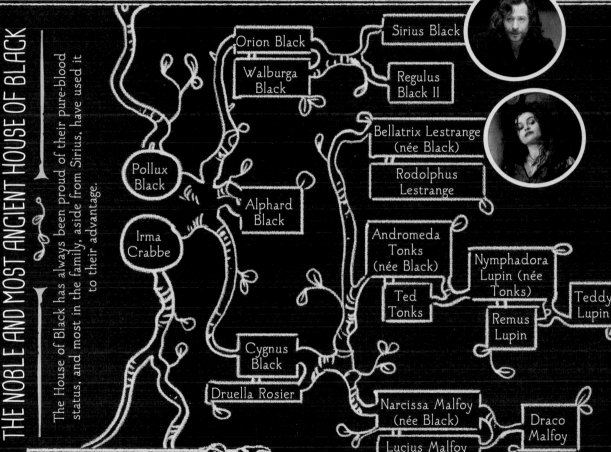

Orion Black
Walburga Black
Sirius Black
Regulus Black II
Pollux Black
Irma Crabbe
Alphard Black
Bellatrix Lestrange (née Black)
Rodolphus Lestrange
Andromeda Tonks (née Black)
Ted Tonks
Nymphadora Lupin (née Tonks)
Remus Lupin
Teddy Lupin
Cygnus Black
Druella Rosier
Narcissa Malfoy (née Black)
Lucius Malfoy
Draco Malfoy

ALL IN THE FAMILY: The Black family tree contains many family names that Wizarding World fans will recognize, such as Crabbe, Rosier, and Lestrange. This is because some ancient wizarding families intermarry to keep the blood lines "pure."

MUGGLES, NO-MAJS, AND SQUIBS

Wizarding communities make up but a microcosm of a larger, more populous world where most cannot perform—or don't even believe in—magic.

In the United Kingdom, Harry Potter's adopted family, the Dursleys, and Hermione Granger's parents are known as MUGGLES—humans who lack the capacity to practice magic and have non-magical parentage on both sides.

NO-MAJ is the American term for Muggle. The aspiring baker Jacob Kowalski is a No-Maj, one of the few who gets a peek at the wonders of magic when his life intersects with Newt Scamander's.

Children who have at least one biological parent with magical blood, yet possess no magical ability themselves, are known as SQUIBS. The caretaker of Hogwarts, Argus Filch, is a Squib, as is Harry Potter's neighbor Arabella Figg.

MAGIC MARRIAGES:

During Harry's time, marriage between Muggles and magic-kind is legal and fairly accepted. But this widespread tolerance wasn't always the case. As we learn in *Fantastic Beasts: The Crimes of Grindelwald*, Queenie wants to marry Jacob, but marriage between magic and non-magic people is illegal in America.

ENEMIES OF MAGIC

The wizarding world may be hidden, but it has not escaped complete notice from those who cannot use magic. Some Muggles and No-Majs fear sorcery and witchcraft and have persecuted wizards and witches over the centuries.

NEW SALEM PHILANTHROPIC SOCIETY (NSPS)

In *Fantastic Beasts and Where to Find Them*, the goal of the NSPS is to warn the non-magical public about the wizards and witches who live among them and the dangers they pose.

The strict and austere MARY LOU BAREBONE leads the NSPS from a church in New York, where she feeds orphans in exchange for distributing her anti-witchcraft pamphlets.

MARY LOU BAREBONE

CHASTITY and MODESTY BAREBONE are two NSPS children who were adopted by Mary Lou Barebone. Chastity is compassionate and kind of heart while dishing out gruel to her fellow orphans. Modesty displays a streak of independence by playing with her toy wand.

CHASTITY

MODESTY

NSPS

WIZARDING PROFESSIONS

Just like Muggles, most witches and wizards have jobs and duties in their various communities.

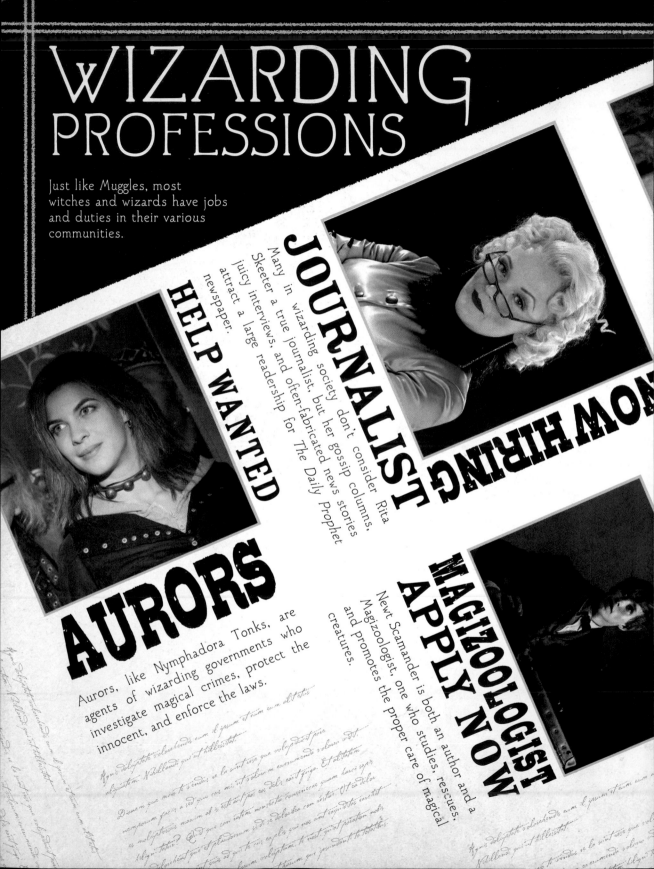

JOURNALIST

Many in wizarding society don't consider Rita Skeeter a true journalist, but her gossip columns, juicy interviews, and often-fabricated news stories attract a large readership for The Daily Prophet newspaper.

NOW HIRING

HELP WANTED

AURORS

Aurors, like Nymphadora Tonks, are agents of wizarding governments who investigate magical crimes, protect the innocent, and enforce the laws.

MAGIZOOLOGIST
APPLY NOW

Newt Scamander, one who studies, rescues, and promotes the proper care of magical creatures. Magizoologist, is both an author and a

ENTREPRENEUR

Many enterprising witches and wizards start their own businesses. Madam Rosmerta owns the Three Broomsticks pub in Hogsmeade, and Fred and George Weasley own Weasleys' Wizard Wheezes in Diagon Alley.

WANDMAKER

Garrick Ollivander is a world-famous Wandmaker. He makes wands, helps witches and wizards find the wand best suited to them, and is sought out for his expertise in understanding how wands work.

OBLIVIATORS

Obliviators, such as Tina and Queenie's coworker Sam, ensure that any No-Majs who witness magical acts have their memories of it erased.

WAND PERMIT OFFICERS

IMMEDIATE OPENING

APPLY NOW

Wand Permit Officers, such as Tina and Queenie Goldstein and their boss, Abernathy, record and maintain the MACUSA registries of wizards and witches who carry wands in the United States.

PART III:
MAGICAL
CREATURES

Of course, magical people aren't the only characters that inhabit the films of the Wizarding World! A large number of magical creatures exist, so much so that an entire course of study at Hogwarts is devoted to learning how to care for such beasts. The films of Harry Potter feature a good number of these creatures, but it's the world of Fantastic Beasts where the true depth of Magizoology is explored.

These playful creatures keep wizards and witches on their toes with all sorts of shenanigans.

Mischief

Tiny BOWTRUCKLES have woody hands and fingers thin enough to pick locks. Newt's Bowtruckle, Pickett, helps Newt out of a pinch or two with his lock-picking abilities!

Pointy-eared CORNISH PIXIES can cause absolute chaos if let loose. Fortunately for the second-year Defense Against the Dark Arts students, Hermione is there with a handy *Immobulus* spell during *Harry Potter and the Chamber of Secrets.*

"WHY IS IT ALWAYS ME?"
—Neville Longbottom

The feline MATAGOT is a spirit familiar somewhat resembling a hairless Sphynx cat. In France, they are utilized by the Minestére des Affaires Magiques de la France to do menial jobs, including staffing the mailroom and providing security for various other departments. Matagots won't attack unless provoked, but then will transform into something far more menacing.

Makers

A bloodsucking creature, the lizard-like CHUPACABRA adores its master—and will sink its fangs into unsuspecting wizards!

NIFFLERS will do anything to sniff out shiny things, like coins, jewelry, buttons, and diamonds, and will pilfer them off one's person before they're ever noticed.

Beware ERUMPENTS in heat: They will stampede through anything, including brick walls, to find their mates.

DRAGONS

Scaled in red and gold, the CHINESE FIREBALL dragon blows balls of fire out of its nostrils. Viktor Krum faces this dragon during the first task of the Triwizard Tournament in *Harry Potter and the Goblet of Fire*.

Cedric Diggory has to find a way to steal an egg from the nest of the yellow-scaled SWEDISH SHORT-SNOUT during his first task in the Triwizard Tournament.

Fleur Delacour has to outsmart the COMMON WELSH GREEN during her first Triwizard Tournament task.

Even the greatest wizards in Harry Potter and Fantastic Beasts fear these FLYING FIREBREATHERS for the destruction they can wreak, although wizards like Newt Scamander, Hagrid, and Charlie Weasley work to ensure these beasts are studied and protected.

Ill-tempered and violent, the black-scaled HUNGARIAN HORNTAIL is considered one of the most dangerous of all dragon breeds and is Harry's dragon to defeat in the Triwizard Tournament.

Newt worked with UKRAINIAN IRONBELLIES, the largest dragon breed in the world, for the Ministry of Magic during the Great War. Harry, Ron, and Hermioane escape Gringotts on the back of a Ukrainian Ironbelly in *Harry Potter and the Deathly Hallows – Part 2.*

The NORWEGIAN RIDGEBACK has brown scales and is not as aggressive as the Hungarian Horntail, though its young can breathe fire at hatching. Hagrid acquires a Norwegian Ridgeback egg, which he successfully hatches in *Harry Potter and the Sorcerer's Stone.* Ron later reveals that his brother Charlie works with this breed in Romania.

Beastly Babies

In Britain, it is illegal to deal in dragon eggs, but Hagrid wins one from a stranger in a pub in *Harry Potter and the Sorcerer's Stone*. Hagrid tries to raise the NORWEGIAN RIDGEBACK that hatches from the egg, naming the dragon baby Norbert, but Hagrid is found out by Draco Malfoy.

Another egg that comes into Hagrid's possession is that of an ACROMANTULA: "Tiny little thing he was when he hatched, no bigger than a Pekingese." Hagrid named the giant spider Aragog and took care of it. Tom Riddle later frames Hagrid and Aragog for the death of Myrtle Warren, as seen in *Harry Potter and the Chamber of Secrets*.

Harry and Luna encounter a young THESTRAL and its parent in the Forbidden Forest during *Harry Potter and the Order of the Phoenix*.

In *Fantastic Beasts and Where to Find Them*, Newt carries an egg that hatches right before his and Jacob Kowalski's eyes in City Bank, revealing a beautiful, iridescent OCCAMY that Newt swiftly nudges inside his case. Newt later tells Jacob that Occamy eggs are quite valuable, as the shells are made of silver.

To Newt's relief, he is able to protect the last breeding pair of GRAPHORNS by hiding them away in his case, ensuring the existence of another Graphorn generation.

Since his exploits in New York, Newt finds himself the keeper of four new baby NIFFLERS, whose father encourages them to sniff out shiny objects.

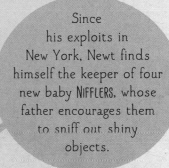

House-elves work for witches and wizards, doing their daily tasks in households and businesses. But these intelligent creatures are more than just servants—they're also as dedicated and loyal a friend as anyone could have.

HANDY HOUSE-ELVES

BAD MASTERS

There are many witches and wizards who abuse house-elves, as we see with Lucius Malfoy in *Harry Potter and the Chamber of Secrets*. Unfortunately, to become a free elf, a witch or wizard must present his or her house-elf with clothes, a rare occurrence.

"YOU LOST ME MY SERVANT!"

WANDLESS WONDERS: House-elves don't typically use wands to cast their magic. A snap of their fingers is enough to accomplish many types of magical feats, including Apparating into/ out of spaces that have Anti-Apparition spells on them.

SNAP!

DOBBY

The Malfoy family mistreats DOBBY, but that doesn't stop him from passing on what he knows about the reopening of the Chamber of Secrets to Harry Potter. After Harry frees Dobby from the Malfoys, the house-elf is forever grateful and promises to do whatever he can to help Harry.

KREACHER

The Black family's house-elf, KREACHER, is not particularly fond of Harry when the young wizard inherits him in Sirius Black's will. Nevertheless, Kreacher does his part to help Harry discover what happened to Salazar Slytherin's locket in *Harry Potter and the Deathly Hallows – Part I.*

HOUSE-ELVES IN 1927

HOUSE-ELVES are seen pouring drinks for Newt Scamander and his friends at The Blind Pig in 1927, while at MACUSA, they can be seen performing jobs like polishing members' wands.

the Basilisk

The Basilisk is regarded as one of the deadliest beasts in the world. A snake of over twenty feet in length, with giant venomous fangs, its status as the king of serpents is well earned.

SNAKE SENTRY: Salazar Slytherin, a founder of Hogwarts, builds the Chamber of Secrets underneath the Hogwarts dungeons and places the Basilisk as its guard.

WATCH OUT: Few have ever gone near the Basilisk and lived to tell the tale. Instant death awaits any who look into one of its eyes.

PETRIFYING: Even those who don't meet the Basilisk's gaze won't have much of a chance. Seeing the Basilisk in a reflection or through other objects, like a camera lens, renders its victims Petrified.

COMMAND WORDS: Only the Heir of Slytherin can command the Basilisk. Tom Riddle speaks in Parseltongue, the language of snakes, to direct the creature to attack Harry Potter.

BURNING DAY: Dumbledore keeps a phoenix named Fawkes on a golden perch in his office. When an elderly phoenix reaches the end of its lifespan, it bursts into flame. And from the ashes emerges a baby phoenix.

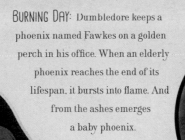

FAWKES TO THE RESCUE: Fawkes comes to Harry Potter's aid in *Harry Potter and the Chamber of Secrets*. After delivering the Sorting Hat for Harry to pull out the Sword of Gryffindor, the bird dives at the Basilisk with its talons and blinds it.

Phoenixes are among the greatest wonders in the magical world. Highly faithful to their masters, they can haul enormous burdens across great distances and their tears can heal wounds.

AVIAN ANTIDOTE: The venom from the Basilisk's bite should have killed Harry, but Fawkes's tears neutralize the poison and save him.

the Phoenix

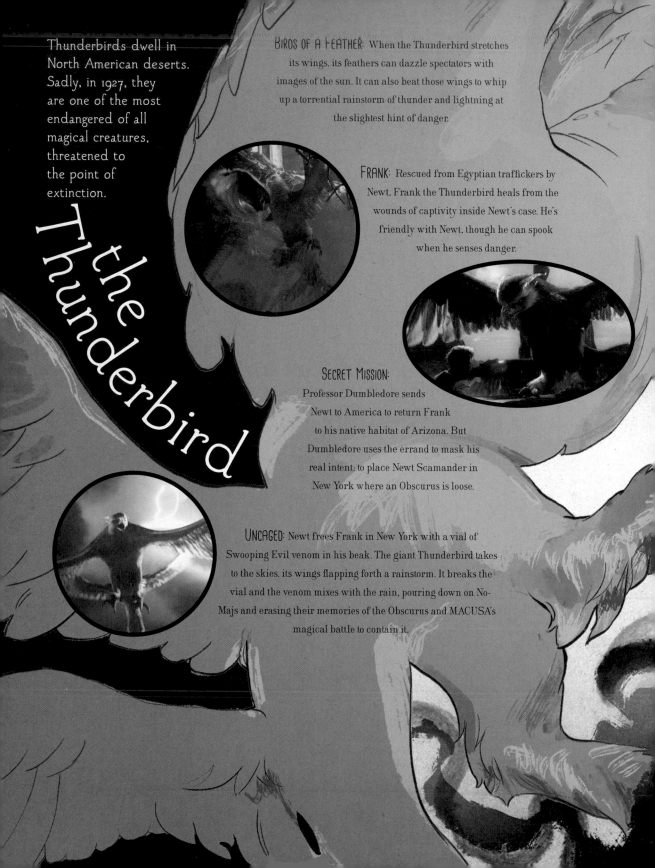

Thunderbirds dwell in North American deserts. Sadly, in 1927, they are one of the most endangered of all magical creatures, threatened to the point of extinction.

the Thunderbird

BIRDS OF A FEATHER: When the Thunderbird stretches its wings, its feathers can dazzle spectators with images of the sun. It can also beat those wings to whip up a torrential rainstorm of thunder and lightning at the slightest hint of danger.

FRANK: Rescued from Egyptian traffickers by Newt, Frank the Thunderbird heals from the wounds of captivity inside Newt's case. He's friendly with Newt, though he can spook when he senses danger.

SECRET MISSION: Professor Dumbledore sends Newt to America to return Frank to his native habitat of Arizona. But Dumbledore uses the errand to mask his real intent: to place Newt Scamander in New York where an Obscurus is loose.

UNCAGED: Newt frees Frank in New York with a vial of Swooping Evil venom in his beak. The giant Thunderbird takes to the skies, its wings flapping forth a rainstorm. It breaks the vial and the venom mixes with the rain, pouring down on No-Majs and erasing their memories of the Obscurus and MACUSA's magical battle to contain it.

OBSCURUS PAST: Obscurials used to be more common prior to Newt's time. Before wizards went underground, they were hunted down by non-magical people. To evade capture, young witches and wizards hid their magic. But these untrained powers boiled inside them, sometimes forming a parasitical entity, or Obscurus, that lashed out at anything around the child, before eventually sucking the child's own life force dry.

CREDENCE BAREBONE: Adopted by Mary Lou Barebone, Credence grows up unloved and is forced to suppress his magical powers. It is this untapped power that has grown into an Obscurus and is expressing its destructive tendencies.

the Obscurus

NEW YORK MENACE: Credence's Obscurus howls through New York City, overturning cars, toppling buildings, tearing up pavement, and causing mayhem wherever it goes. Part of its power is due to Credence's age—most Obscurials never make it past childhood. But in *Fantastic Beasts: The Crimes of Grindelwald*, Credence is slowly learning to control this Dark force.

Those who have seen the Obscurus and lived to talk about it describe it as a gust of wind, a shadow, or a dark cloud. It is a violent force of chaos manifested from an Obscurial, a youth with magical blood who is forced to repress his or her magic.

NEWT'S CASE: Newt has another Obscurus in his case. He captured it in Africa after it took the life of an eight-year-old Sudanese girl.

CREATURES at HOGWARTS

The GROUNDS OF HOGWARTS are home to a number of magical creatures, as both Newt and Harry discover during their time there.

Beneath the cold waters of the Black Lake lives a colony of MERPEOPLE, an intelligent species with humanlike upper bodies and the silvery tails of fish. They have mouths full of sharp teeth, and they will jab their spears at anyone who threatens their depths, as Harry learns during the second task of the Triwizard Tournament.

BLACK LAKE

GRINDYLOWS are stumpy green water devils who inhabit the seaweed beds of the Black Lake. They catch their prey with their tentacles and once nearly drowned Harry in *Harry Potter and the Goblet of Fire*. Fortunately, Remus Lupin had taught Harry how to repel them the year before.

Though rarely seen in the Forest, UNICORNS are highly revered. These sleek, white equines bear a single horn on their heads, and their blood can "keep you alive even if you are an inch from death."

CASTLE

Hagrid keeps Buckbeak, his HIPPOGRIFF, near his hut just outside the castle. Hippogriffs are generally calm unless provoked by insults, which they will respond to with squawking, unbridled fury.

Harry, Ron, and Hermione encounter their first MOUNTAIN TROLL in the girls' bathroom in *Harry Potter and the Sorcerer's Stone*. Cleverness may not be one of the species' chief attributes, but its brawn more than makes up for what it lacks in brains.

A three-headed dog named FLUFFY once guarded the entrance to the hiding place of the Sorcerer's Stone. Though the dog's name sounds cute and cuddly, he can be anything but—and for those who intrude on the premises, his bite is even worse than his bark.

Travelers who veer off the paths should watch out for ACROMANTULAS like Aragog. These giant spiders spin webs in the Forest's trees, hollows, and caves, and relish eating humans. They can even speak to victims trapped in their webs!

FORBIDDEN FOREST

A herd of CENTAURS protects the Forest from unwanted intruders. These proud creatures have the head, arms, and torso of a human, and the body and legs of a horse. Devoted stargazers, they are skilled in divining the future. Harry Potter is rescued by the Centaur Firenze in *Harry Potter and the Sorcerer's Stone*, and the herd later drives Dolores Umbridge off the grounds in Harry's fifth year.

Rubeus Hagrid, as the Keeper of Keys and Grounds at Hogwarts, oversees the care of the THESTRALS in the Forest. Thestrals pull the carriages that take students from the Hogwarts Express to the castle after their first year.

GIANTS

GIANTS are tall—*really* tall—sometimes over twenty-five feet. They can range from looking like oversized, hairy humans to bald and mottled trolls.

GIANT FAMILIES:

Though rare, giants and humans have fallen in love, producing half-giant offspring like RUBEUS HAGRID. The headmistress of Beauxbatons Academy in France, MADAME OLYMPE MAXIME, is also a half-giant like Hagrid. During Bill and Fleur's wedding in *Harry Potter and the Deathly Hallows – Part 1*, Hagrid can be seen smiling at Olympe's side.

In *Harry Potter and the Order of the Phoenix*, Dumbledore sends Hagrid to find giants to support the Order of the Phoenix. Hagrid isn't successful in recruiting the giants, but he does bring back his half-brother, GRAWP. Grawp is a full-blood giant, and Hagrid keeps him in the Forbidden Forest, where he asks Harry, Ron, and Hermione to look out for his brother should anything happen to him.

"GRAWP! PUT ME DOWN!"

BIG FUN: During Newt's adventures in New York, one can spot a giant enjoying a beverage at The Blind Pig speakeasy.

GOBLINS

Goblins are small beings with humanoid features, long pointy ears and noses, and very sharp minds. Like house-elves, they perform their own version of wandless magic.

Goblins make excellent metalsmiths—the Sword of Gryffindor is an example of their trade, as GRIPHOOK tells Harry in *Harry Potter and the Deathly Hallows – Part 2*, but they also make great money managers. Their species runs Gringotts bank, which supervises the flow of money and keeps the economy of the British wizarding community humming.

The goblin GNARLAK isn't a banker like most of his kin, rather he's an information broker who sometimes illegally trades in magical creatures. He owns and operates The Blind Pig speakeasy in Manhattan, where he trades in the secrets that are spilled at his bar.

WEREWOLVES

Werewolves are humans infected with lycanthropy, which forces their bodies to transform into a wolf whenever there is a full moon. They are not to be confused with ANIMAGI, who can transform into a different creature at will.

FENRIR GREYBACK is a vicious werewolf who joins Lord Voldemort's Death Eaters to help the Dark Lord retake what he lost in the First Wizarding War.

REMUS LUPIN is one of James Potter's friends who helped create the Marauder's Map. He suffers from lycanthropy but later becomes a professor at Hogwarts and keeps his secret from his students.

CIRCUS ARCANUS

In *Fantastic Beasts: The Crimes of Grindelwald*, all kinds of magical acts are on display in Skender's CIRCUS ARCANUS, from the curious to the strange, and all are mistreated by Skender. Many of these acts are referred to as UNDERBEINGS—those with wizarding ancestry but who lack magical powers.

NO FLINT NECESSARY
FIREDRAKES
CAN SPARK YOUR FIRE!

FIREDRAKES'
SPARKS CAN IGNITE FLAMES. WHEN CREDENCE ESCAPES THE CIRCUS, HE LETS THEM OUT OF THEIR CAGE AND SOON THE BIG TOP IS AFLAME.

ARCANUS
MUSÉE DES CURIOSITÉS VIVANTES

No 11 No 11279
CIRQUE
CIF
TICKET D'ENTRÉE!
TICKET
ADMISSION
POUR UNE PERSONNE
POUR UN: ENFANT
ARCANUS
MUSÉE DES CURIOSITÉS VIVANTES

LE PLUS GRAND DES CIRQUES
L'ÉVEMENT DU SIÈCLE!
PRIX
SEULEMENT POUR LE SPECTACLE
D'AUJOURD'HUI!
Véritable!
ADULTES 5 bz
Stupéfiant!
ENFANTS 2 ¾ bz
Ouvert tous les soirs à 8 hres
MATINÉES MAGIQUES ENFANTINES 3 hres
Les Jeudis et Dimanches

LE CIRQUE ARCANUS

M̲USÉE
CUR...
VIV...

IS SHE A BEAUTIFUL WOMAN... OR IS SHE A BEAST?

THE MALEDICTUS IS A PERSON WHO CARRIES A BLOOD CURSE THAT, OVER THE COURSE OF HIS OR HER LIFE, WILL TURN THEM PERMANENTLY INTO A BEAST.

UNDER NEWT'S PROTECTION

The sagacious **DEMIGUISE** gave Newt quite a chase when it got loose in a New York department store in *Fantastic Beasts and Where to Find Them*. Not only can it turn invisible, but its precognition gives it the ability to predict the next actions Newt and his friends will take with remarkable accuracy.

The plumed **OCCAMY** has a unique ability called choranaptyxis, meaning it is able to transform its size to fit whatever space it occupies, whether it be a large room or a tiny teapot.

The massive, lion-like **NUNDU** is also a resident of Newt's case.

NEWT SCAMANDER'S CASE and the BASEMENT of his London flat contain another world in and of itself, full of endangered or injured beasts he's rescued and the environments in which they dwell.

Don't judge a FWOOPER by its size— these small birds can consume a big piece of meat in one swallow.

Jacob Kowalski wonders at the massive DUNG BEETLES that march around Newt's shed.

The MURTLAP is a squirmy creature and very hard to wrangle with its tentacles. Its bite gives No-Majs a nasty rash, as Jacob learned in *Fantastic Beasts and Where to Find Them.*

A family of GRAPHORNS live in Newt's case, and they welcome the Magizoologist by wrapping his head and shoulders in their tentacles. The breeding pair have two young offspring.

UNDER NEWT'S PROTECTION

The docile MOONCALVES, with their enormous eyes, live in a dark meadow in Newt's case where only moonlight shines.

Fat, feathered, and flightless, one can see a flock of DIRICAWL BIRDS running through Newt's case.

Among the many creatures that escape Newt's case in New York are BILLYWIGS, which zip through the air with wings on the heads of their insect bodies.

A luminescent GLOW BUG, as well as the aforementioned GRINDYLOW, can be seen "bubbled" alongside the OBSCURUS in Newt's case.

When the SWOOPING EVIL emerges from its cocoon, it can be a frightening sight. With help from the Swooping Evil, Newt and Tina escape executioners at MACUSA, and later apprehend Grindelwald. Swooping Evil venom can help remove undesired memories.

In his basement, Newt has a huge pool for his KELPIE, a horse-like water creature that gives Bunty a hard time. Newt uses a bridle to get a handle on the Kelpie long enough to apply ointment to an injury.

A pair of winged DOXIES circle around Jacob's head as he explores Newt's case in *Fantastic Beasts and Where to Find Them.*

Newt also is tending to a beautiful, sad-looking bird known as an AUGUREY in his basement.

BOGGARTS

RON WEASLEY'S fear of spiders is well-known from his run-in with Aragog. Ron adds roller skates to defeat his Boggart.

NEVILLE LONGBOTTOM'S greatest fear in his third year was Professor Snape. It was Professor Lupin's idea to imagine him in Neville's grandmother's clothes.

PARVATI PATIL is afraid of snakes. Her *Riddikulus* transforms the snake into a jack-in-the-box.

BOGGARTS are magical creatures that will shapeshift into one's greatest fear. For this reason, no one actually knows what a Boggart looks like when it's alone. Boggarts tend to hide in enclosed spaces like closets and cupboards and can be difficult to get rid of. The only way to make a Boggart disappear is to laugh at it. For this reason, witches and wizards cast the *Riddikulus* spell, which turns the Boggart into something funny. As we see in both *Harry Potter and the Prisoner of Azkaban* and *Fantastic Beasts: The Crimes of Grindelwald*, Hogwarts students typically learn about Boggarts and how to combat them in their Defense Against the Dark Arts classes.

HARRY POTTER is never given the chance to cast Riddikulus on his Boggart in class. Instead, Professor Lupin uses a Boggart, which transforms into a Dementor for Harry, to teach him about the Patronus Charm.

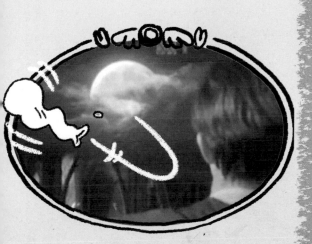

As a werewolf, REMUS LUPIN'S greatest fear was the full moon. He turned the moon into a deflating balloon.

NEWT SCAMANDER'S Boggart is a bit more abstract than his classmates —it's being trapped in a career and life he doesn't want. Newt's greatest fear is spending his life working in an office.

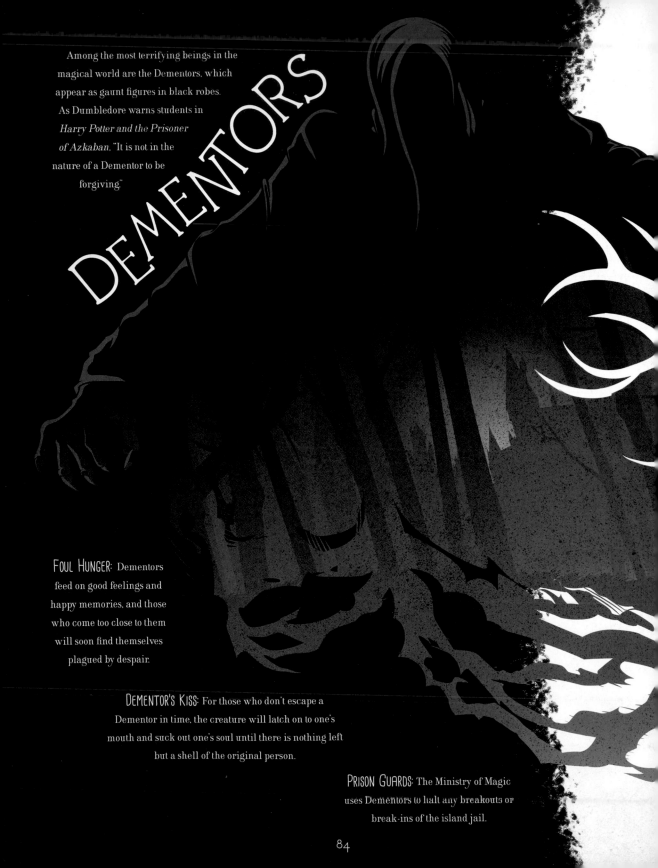

Among the most terrifying beings in the magical world are the Dementors, which appear as gaunt figures in black robes. As Dumbledore warns students in *Harry Potter and the Prisoner of Azkaban*, "It is not in the nature of a Dementor to be forgiving."

DEMENTORS

FOUL HUNGER: Dementors feed on good feelings and happy memories, and those who come too close to them will soon find themselves plagued by despair.

DEMENTOR'S KISS: For those who don't escape a Dementor in time, the creature will latch on to one's mouth and suck out one's soul until there is nothing left but a shell of the original person.

PRISON GUARDS: The Ministry of Magic uses Dementors to halt any breakouts or break-ins of the island jail.

PATRONUSES

BEST DEFENSE: Dementors aren't able to be killed in the traditional sense, since they are not living creatures. But a Patronus Charm can ward them off. This can be a complicated charm to conjure, but if successful, it summons a guardian spirit that can drive away Dementors.

Ron Weasley

Hermione Granger

Luna Lovegood

Ginny Weasley

HARRY'S PATRONUS:

Patronus guardians manifest in particular forms suited to each spellcaster. Harry Potter's Patronus takes the shape of a stag, which was his father's Animagus form.

OTHER PATRONUSES:

Severus Snape

Lily Potter

Dolores Umbridge

PART IV:
MAGICAL
OBJECTS

From enchanted games to cursed necklaces, magical maps to unique inventions, the films of the Wizarding World are awash with one-of-a-kind wonders. Who wouldn't want a mirror that could show you your heart's greatest desire? Or a set of relics that could make one Master of Death? In this section, you'll find the most incredible magical objects that Harry, Newt, and their companions encounter.

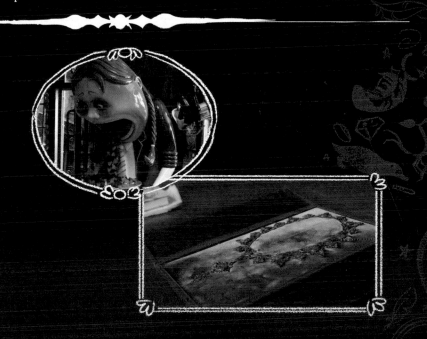

WANDS

Wands are the conduits of a wizard or witch's magic, the most important tool for wizardkind.

HARRY has a wand that shares a Phoenix-feather core from the same Phoenix as Lord Voldemort's wand. In Harry's fourth year at Hogwarts, this causes a strange phenomenon known as *Priori Incantatem*, in which Harry's wand forces the Dark Lord's wand to reproduce the most recent spells it has performed.

LORD VOLDEMORT abandons his original wand in *Harry Potter and the Deathly Hallows – Part 1*, taking Lucius Malfoy's wand instead. Lucius's wand breaks during a duel with Harry, at which point the Dark Lord sets his sights on the Elder Wand.

HERMIONE is an incredibly talented spellcaster, executing many spells flawlessly from her first year at Hogwarts.

RON buys this wand after his first wand broke during a run-in with the Whomping Willow.

WAND BREAKING: When a wand breaks, it is essentially dead. As Ron learns in *Harry Potter and the Chamber of Secrets*, spells cast by a broken wand will typically bounce back at the spellcaster.

TINA battles with Grindelwald as the Obscurus tears through New York's streets. She casts her spells with very little flourishing of her wand.

QUEENIE, on the other hand, is very artistic with her magic. When preparing dinner for Tina, Newt, and Jacob, she runs the kitchen like a symphony, preparing a strudel from scratch before their eyes.

WANDCRAFTING: Wood from trees such as cedar, holly, and elm make strong wand shafts that help channel magic. A magical core, such as a dragon heartstring or a unicorn hair, is set inside the wand to capture and focus the wizard's or witch's magic.

GRINDELWALD often displays his incredible power without the use of a wand. In *Fantastic Beasts and Where to Find Them*, he disarms and restrains Newt, Tina, and Jacob with nothing more than a wave of his hand.

NEWT often pairs his spell-casting with help from his creatures. When he and Tina escape the MACUSA Aurors, and when they ultimately apprehend Grindelwald, Newt combines well-timed charms with back-up from a Swooping Evil

WIZARDS AND WANDS: Wands can be purchased from wandmakers like Ollivander or can be won in duels with other wizards. But the wand must have an affinity for the one who holds it to produce the magic the spellcaster wants. There's truth to Garrick Ollivander's words: "The wand chooses the wizard."

Magical Fashion in Fantastic Beasts

PRESIDENTIAL FINERY: When she addresses MACUSA, President Seraphina Picquery wears a tailored black gown and floral headpiece, both filigreed in gold.

TRENDSETTER: Queenie Goldstein doesn't need to shop with her dressmaking spells. Magazines such as *The Witch's Friend* keep her up to date on the latest styles.

PERSONAL STYLE: Newt Scamander's peacock-blue overcoat provides both function and flair. He dons a similar, though less conspicuous, gray overcoat during his time in London and Paris.

Fashion is all the rage in the ROARING TWENTIES, on both sides of the Atlantic.

MAGICAL MODE: Tina and Queenie transform their drab day clothes into sparkling party dresses as they enter The Blind Pig with Newt and Jacob.

Magical Fashion in Harry Potter

CHRISTMAS DANCE: For the Yule Ball in *Harry Potter and the Goblet of Fire*, students from each competing school dress to impress. Many of the witches wear gowns that accentuate their traits, while the wizards try to look dapper in stylish robes. Hermione's showstopper tiered gown turned heads.

HOGWARTS UNIFORMS THROUGH THE AGES

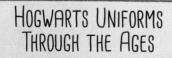

1920s

Boys and girls wear robes with a chain clasp closure and three stripes on the sleeves. House crest is emblazoned on the robes. Sweaters with house-color detailing and house-color ties are worn. Girls wear plaid skirts.

1930s-40s

Pupils wear gray blazers with house emblems over a white shirt, tie, and gray or black sweater. Cloaks closely resemble those worn in the 1920s, but without the chain clasp closure or the striped sleeves.

DUMBLEDORE'S GOT STYLE: The many incredible robes worn by Albus Dumbledore are not to be overlooked, with sumptuous fabrics, trims, and accessories befitting a headmaster.

REGAL ROBES: Kingsley Shacklebolt's colorful Agbada robes and cap reflect his African heritage, with color-changing silk as well as intricate beads and embroidery.

REQUIRED DRESS: Hogwarts mandates that students follow the uniform dress code during instructional periods, study halls, dining hours, and school events. They may wear casual clothes only during free time.

1970S–80S   1990S   2000

Similar to 1930s–40s. Button closure is added to cloaks.

Blazers are eliminated. Students wear white shirts, gray sweaters, and ties showing their house colors under plain black robes. Female students may wear black pants or a gray or black skirt. Prefects and students who have an assigned duty wear badges on their robes.

HOGWARTS

ARTIFACTS

Countless objects with unique, magical properties have found their way to Hogwarts, including several that have become legendary.

"NOT SLYTHERIN . . . NOT SLYTHERIN."

THE SORTING HAT

is kept in the headmaster's office and brought out during the start-of-term feast each year. The hat is placed on each new student's head in the Great Hall, and reads the young wearer until it announces which of the four houses that student will join. Though, as we see in *Harry Potter and the Sorcerer's Stone*, the hat does take into consideration what house the wearer wants to join.

PENSIEVE

Ancients runes are carved around the basin of the PENSIEVE, which allows those who look into it to view memories. Dumbledore keeps the Pensieve in his office, and to access it, one must flip a switch in the floor.

MIRROR OF ERISED

To look into the MIRROR OF ERISED is to see a reflection of one's heart's desire. Harry Potter discovers it in an unused classroom during his first year and returns to it multiple times to behold the faces of his parents. The mirror appears again in *Fantastic Beasts: The Crimes of Grindelwald*.

SWORD OF GRYFFINDOR

Forged by goblins a thousand years ago for Godric Gryffindor himself, the Sword of Gryffindor can only be wielded by a true Gryffindor. Harry uses it to slay the Basilisk in the Chamber of Secrets; later, Ron and Neville use it to destroy two of Voldemort's Horcruxes.

GOBLET OF FIRE

Before the Triwizard Tournament officially commences, potential participants place their names, written on a slip of parchment, into the GOBLET OF FIRE. The Goblet then spits out from the flames the name of a single student from each school to compete. In *Harry Potter and the Goblet of Fire*, however, the Goblet selects two students from Hogwarts, due to a Confundus Charm cast upon it by Barty Crouch Jr.

THE DELUMINATOR

The Deluminator captures any surrounding lights and then restores them if wanted. Albus Dumbledore uses it to darken the lights when he meets Newt Scamander in London in *Fantastic Beasts: The Crimes of Grindelwald*. Many years later, in *Harry Potter and the Sorcerer's Stone*, he uses it again to extinguish the streetlights around Privet Drive. After his death, the Deluminator is bequeathed to Ron, who discovers another of its hidden powers: It can unleash a ball of light that guides one to the place they need to be.

STRANGE
SIGHTS

Of course, unique artifacts aren't rare to Hogwarts. Witches and wizards have been inventing incredible magical objects for centuries.

MARAUDER'S MAP

Those who wish to visit every nook and cranny of Hogwarts, or even track the various occupants, need look no further than the MARAUDER'S MAP. A band of students known as the Marauders created the map before Harry's time, and not without a sense of humor. The map dishes out insults to those who don't know the phrase to activate it, as Snape learns in *Harry Potter and the Prisoner of Azkaban*. To open the map, one must say, "I solemnly swear that I am up to no good," and close the map by saying, "Mischief managed" when finished.

" I SOLEMNLY SWEAR THAT I AM UP TO NO GOOD."

WIZARD CHESS

WIZARD CHESS is like the non-wizarding version of the game, except that the players' pieces move on their own and physically attack the opposing pieces. Ron Weasley is an expert at the game and applies his skills to the giant chessboard obstacle he faces in *Harry Potter and the Sorcerer's Stone*.

VANISHING CABINETS

A pair of VANISHING CABINETS allows a person to enter one cabinet and exit the other, wherever it is located. As Arthur Weasley tells Harry in *Harry Potter and the Half-Blood Prince*, "They were all the rage when Voldemort first rose to power." Draco uses the Vanishing Cabinet at Borgin and Burkes to sneak Death Eaters inside Hogwarts.

THE SORCERER'S STONE

The SORCERER'S STONE produces a fluid known as the Elixir of Life, which transmutes metal into gold, but also lengthens the lifespan of anyone who drinks it. Nicolas Flamel, the centuries-old alchemist, is its only known maker. In his first year at Hogwarts, Harry procures the Stone to keep it from Lord Voldemort, and Dumbledore later tells Harry that he and Flamel agreed to destroy it. However, one can also catch a glimpse of the famous stone in Flamel's home in *Fantastic Beasts: The Crimes of Grindelwald*.

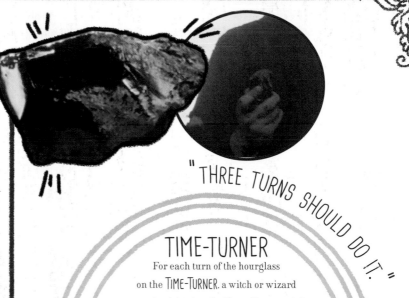

"THREE TURNS SHOULD DO IT."

TIME-TURNER

For each turn of the hourglass on the TIME-TURNER, a witch or wizard can go back in time. In *Harry Potter and the Prisoner of Azkaban*, Professor McGonagall gives one to Hermione Granger so she can attend additional classes above and beyond her regular schedule. But as Hermione tells Harry, "Awful things happen to wizards who meddle with time." When Harry and Hermione use the Time-Turner to save Sirius Black and Buckbeak, they are extremely careful not to be seen.

WEASLEY CLOCK

Don't rely on the WEASLEY CLOCK in Ron's home for the time. The nine gray hands on the clock track the activities and whereabouts of each of the nine family members, from the "Dentist" to "Mortal Peril."

CRYSTAL BALL

Of the many artifacts in Nicolas Flamel's home, one of the most unique is the CRYSTAL BALL that lets him glimpse what is happening in different places, as we see in *Fantastic Beasts: The Crimes of Grindelwald*.

MERRY PRANKSTERS

Some of the most incredible objects in the wizarding world are invented not from hard study, but from . . . extra-curricular pursuits. FRED AND GEORGE WEASLEY spin their genius prank inventions into a successful business, WEASLEYS' WIZARD WHEEZES, which can fulfill every mischief-maker's wildest dreams!

WHAT PRANK CAN WEASLEYS' WIZARD WHEEZES HELP YOU WITH?

A SWEET TO HELP YOU GET OUT OF CLASS

A PRANK WITH SOME BOOM

HELP WITH A RECONNAISSANCE MISSION

PUKING PASTILLES DO, WELL, EXACTLY WHAT THE NAME IMPLIES!

FEVER FUDGE GIVES THE USER A HIGH FEVER AND PUS-FILLED BOILS. FRED AND GEORGE TEST THESE ON ARGUS FILCH IN *HARRY POTTER AND THE ORDER OF THE PHOENIX*.

FAINTING FANCIES WILL CAUSE THE CONSUMER TO PASS OUT—ONE CAN BE WOKEN BY EATING THE ANTIDOTE IN THE BOX.

NOSEBLEED NOUGAT CREATES A MASSIVE NOSEBLEED SURE TO SEND YOU HOME FROM SCHOOL!

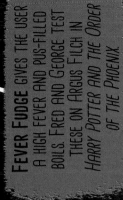

WILDFIRE WHIZ-BANGS ARE A COMPLETE FIREWORKS SHOW IN A BOX. JUST MAKE SURE YOU HAVE LOTS OF ROOM TO SET THEM OFF ....

DUNGBOMBS OFFER AN EXPLOSION OF SMELL. THESE PRANKS ARE A CLASSIC—LETA LESTRANGE RECALLS SETTING ONE OFF WITH NEWT SCAMANDER DURING THEIR YEARS AT HOGWARTS NEARLY A CENTURY AGO IN *FANTASTIC BEASTS: THE CRIMES OF GRINDELWALD*.

PERUVIAN INSTANT DARKNESS POWDER IS IDEAL WHEN YOU HAVE TO MAKE A QUICK GETAWAY.

EXTENDABLE EARS ARE PERFECT FOR EAVESDROPPING!

WIZARDING NEWS

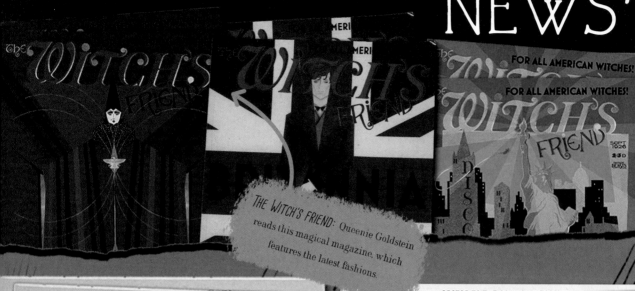

THE WITCH'S FRIEND: Queenie Goldstein reads this magical magazine, which features the latest fashions.

NEW YORK GHOST: America's national wizarding newspaper publishes two daily editions. An annual subscription costs five Dragots.

LE CRI DE LA GARGOUILLE: Reports the wizarding news in France.

THE WIZARD'S VOICE: This competitor to the New York Ghost is geared toward the "common wizard," per its slogan.

News travels fast through the wizarding world, and while some listen to the radio station, WIZARDING WIRELESS NETWORK, many witches and wizards still prefer to get their news in print. Witches and wizards can pick up these publications at newsstands or order a subscription to have them delivered by OWL POST.

THE QUIBBLER: Not widely respected for its sensational coverage, the *Quibbler* still maintains a small and loud following for those interested in weird news. It is edited by Luna Lovegood's father, Xenophilius.

WITCH WEEKLY: This weekly magazine awarded Gilderoy Lockhart their "Most Charming Smile" award five times.

TRANSFIGURATION TODAY: Albus Dumbledore wrote an article for this academic journal, which can be seen in *Fantastic Beasts and Where to Find Them*.

THE DAILY PROPHET: The most influential wizarding newspaper in Great Britain. At the request of the Ministry of Magic, it runs a slanderous campaign against Harry in *Harry Potter and the Order of the Phoenix*, insisting that Lord Voldemort has not returned.

Wizarding books aren't just ink and parchment—magic animates the pages as well. Harry and Newt visit several bookstores in the wizarding world, though perhaps the best known is FLOURISH AND BLOTTS.

BOOKS

VOLUME 5

ADVANCED
DADA
DEFENCE AGAINST
THE DARK ARTS

DEFENSE AGAINST THE DARK ARTS
Students of Albus Dumbledore's 1927 classes used these textbooks in *Fantastic Beasts: The Crimes of Grindelwald*.

FANTASTIC BEASTS AND WHERE TO FIND THEM BY NEWT SCAMANDER
The classic textbook of magical creatures, written by Newt and later read by Harry Potter as part of his studies at Hogwarts. Newt has mixed feelings about the book during *Fantastic Beasts: The Crimes of Grindelwald*. On the one hand, it educates the wizarding world about the need to protect creatures; on the other hand, it made him more famous than he ever wanted to be.

BESTIARIVM
MAGICVM

NEWT SCAMANDER
FANTASTIC
BEASTS
AND WHERE TO FIND THEM

BESTIARIUM MAGICUM
A compendium of magical beasts, which Newt keeps in his case for reference.

ADVANCED POTION-MAKING
BY LIBATIUS BORAGE
The textbook for sixth-year Potions students. Harry's copy was annotated by Severus Snape, who called himself the HALF-BLOOD PRINCE.

BOOK SIGNING: The films of the Wizarding World feature two book signing events at Flourish and Blotts. Images of Newt signing copies of his book can be seen in *Fantastic Beasts: The Crimes of Grindelwald*. Many years later, Gilderoy Lockhart does a book signing in *Harry Potter and the Chamber of Secrets*.

THE MONSTER BOOK OF MONSTERS
Another popular textbook for CARE OF MAGICAL CREATURES. As Hagrid warns his class in *Harry Potter and the Prisoner of Azkaban*, one must stroke the spine to open the book, or it will bite.

SPELLMAN'S SYLLABARY
A textbook used in Ancient Runes class.

TRAVELS WITH TROLLS
Gilderoy Lockhart wrote many books about his supposed great deeds.

SECRETS OF THE DARKEST ART
A medieval manuscript that includes Dark Magic; TOM RIDDLE used this book to learn how to create a HORCRUX.

THE TALES OF BEEDLE THE BARD
A collection of fairy tales for young witches and wizards. Dumbledore bequeathed his copy to Hermione after his death; it contains "THE TALE OF THE THREE BROTHERS," the origin story for the DEATHLY HALLOWS.

KEEP IN TOUCH!

Throughout the films, the wizarding world stays connected with various methods of magical communication.

The OWL POST is the tried and true method of delivery in the wizarding world. Owls carry messages sent from an Owl Post Office to their intended recipient.

Individuals also keep OWLS to make personal deliveries. For Harry's eleventh birthday, Hagrid gives Harry a snowy owl that Harry names Hedwig. She not only carries his post to friends, but she is also a loyal friend herself. He keeps her in the Owlery at Hogwarts with the other owls.

NICOLAS FLAMEL possesses a magical book that lets him converse with other wizards.

WATCH OUT

—not all mail is good news. Once opened, the aptly named HOWLER bursts out, in the booming voice of its author the words of the angry letter inside. Trying to ignore a Howler is of no use—upon delivery, it will howl the contents of the letter to everyone in its vicinity, as Ron learns in *Harry Potter and the Chamber of Secrets.*

In addition to transportation, the FLOO NETWORK provides face-to-face conversation over distances. By using Floo Powder in a fireplace, a wizard or witch can transport their head or voice to another fireplace in the network. Sirius Black employed this method on multiple occasions when talking to Harry Potter during Harry's fourth and fifth years at Hogwarts.

Experienced wizards can also use their PATRONUS to deliver secret messages of the utmost importance. Through his Patronus, Kingsley Shacklebolt, an Auror of the Ministry of Magic and a member of the Order of the Phoenix, warns guests at Bill and Fleur's wedding that the Ministry of Magic has fallen to Voldemort during *Harry Potter and the Deathly Hallows – Part 1.*

DARK OBJECTS

The darkest of the Dark Arts is the creation of a HORCRUX, an object or being in which a wizard or witch stores a sliver of his or her soul to achieve never-ending life.

HORCRUX CREATION:

As Slughorn reveals to Tom Riddle in *Harry Potter and the Half-Blood Prince*, murder is necessary in creating a Horcrux, followed by the casting of a spell to tear part of the soul from the spellcaster and place it within a desired object. When that is completed, the wizard or witch cannot die unless the Horcrux is destroyed.

HORCRUX DESTRUCTION:

Lord Voldemort cast powerful protection spells to make it near impossible to destroy his Horcruxes. It takes special objects and substances, such as Basilisk venom, to penetrate the container and cause the Horcrux to "bleed" out the soul trapped inside.

TOM RIDDLE'S DIARY

Harry Potter drives a venomous Basilisk fang through its pages.

MARVOLO GAUNT'S RING

Albus Dumbledore destroys it with the Sword of Gryffindor.

SALAZAR SLYTHERIN'S LOCKET

Ron Weasley smashes it with the Sword of Gryffindor.

OTHER DARK ARTIFACTS

DOLORES UMBRIDGE punishes students by making them write with the **BLACK QUILL**. The pen etches whatever is written with it into the user's skin.

The **IMPERIUS CURSE** cast on Katie Bell forces her to pick up a package containing an **OPAL NECKLACE**. She is supposed to bring the necklace to Albus Dumbledore, but when she touches the necklace accidentally, it nearly kills her.

Harry stabs the diadem with a Basilisk fang, before Ron kicks it into a plume of Fiendfyre in the Room of Requirement.

Neville Longbottom chops off the head of Lord Voldemort's beloved snake with the Sword Gryffindo

ROWENA RAVENCLAW'S DIADEM

VOLDEMORT'S HORCRUXES:

Over the years, Tom Riddle creates seven different Horcruxes and divides his soul among them. To end his reign of terror and his immortality, all Horcruxes must be destroyed.

NAGINI

Hermione Granger plunges a Basilisk fang into its metal.

HELGA HUFFLEPUFF'S CUP

SEVENTH HORCRUX HARRY POTTER:

Voldemort's murder of Harry's parents is such a terrible crime that some of Voldemort's soul breaks off and attaches itself to Harry Potter. This makes Harry Potter a Horcrux as well, though Harry doesn't fully realize it until late in the Battle of Hogwarts. Lord Voldemort destroys the Horcrux when he casts the Killing Curse on Harry in the Forbidden Forest; Harry survives, but the Horcrux does not.

DEATHLY

A trio of magical artifacts are known as the DEATHLY HALLOWS. It is said that the one who acquires and unites these objects will become the MASTER OF DEATH. Harry Potter and Albus Dumbledore are the only known people to have been in possession of all three Hallows, though neither had all of them at the same time.

As told in "THE TALE OF THE THREE BROTHERS," the three Peverell brothers conjure a bridge over a treacherous river that would have otherwise taken their lives. Feeling swindled, Death appears before them, asking how he can reward them for their ingenuity. The eldest brother is given the most powerful of all wands, the ELDER WAND. The second brother wishes to resurrect the dead, and Death provides him with the RESURRECTION STONE. The youngest brother asks for something to hide him from Death, and rather reluctantly, Death makes a CLOAK OF INVISIBILITY.

THE SIGN OF THE DEATHLY HALLOWS CAN BE SEEN IN MANY PLACES IN THE FILMS:

Decoration on Marvolo Gaunt's ring, worn by both Dumbledore and Tom Riddle

Grave of Ignotus Peverell

Grindelwald, disguised as Percival Graves, wears a pendant bearing the symbol, which he gives to Credence.

Emblem on Xenophilius Lovegood's necklace

Inscription in Dumbledore's copy of *The Tales of Beedle the Bard*

HALLOWS

KNOWN MASTERS OF THE ELDER WAND

Antioch Peverell,
eldest Peverell
brother

Gregorovitch

Gellert Grindelwald

Albus Dumbledore

Draco Malfoy

Lord Voldemort
(though he was never
its true master,
as he had not
disarmed Draco)

Harry Potter, who
ultimately destroys
the wand

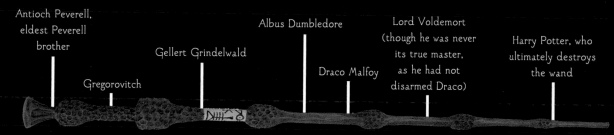

THE ELDER WAND is the most powerful wand. It is undefeatable in battle, so long as the wielder has disarmed or murdered the previous wielder. It is made from elder wood with a Thestral-tail-hair core, and is fifteen inches long.

By turning the RESURRECTION STONE over three times, the one who holds it can summon the spirits of the dead. It is hidden in the Golden Snitch that Dumbledore gives Harry Potter upon his death. Harry uses it to summon the spirits of his departed loved ones before he faces Lord Voldemort in the Forbidden Forest.

The CLOAK OF INVISIBILITY causes its wearer to disappear from sight. It was passed down in Harry's family from his father, James, to Harry himself.

PART V:
MAGIC

The sights, people, creatures, and objects that make up the films of the Wizarding World are quite wondrous, but nothing is quite so incredible as the magic that keeps the films themselves turning. In this section, you'll find more information about many ways that charms, curses, potions, and plants make the Wizarding World even more magical.

SPELLS IN HARRY POTTER'S FIRST FOUR YEARS AT HOGWARTS

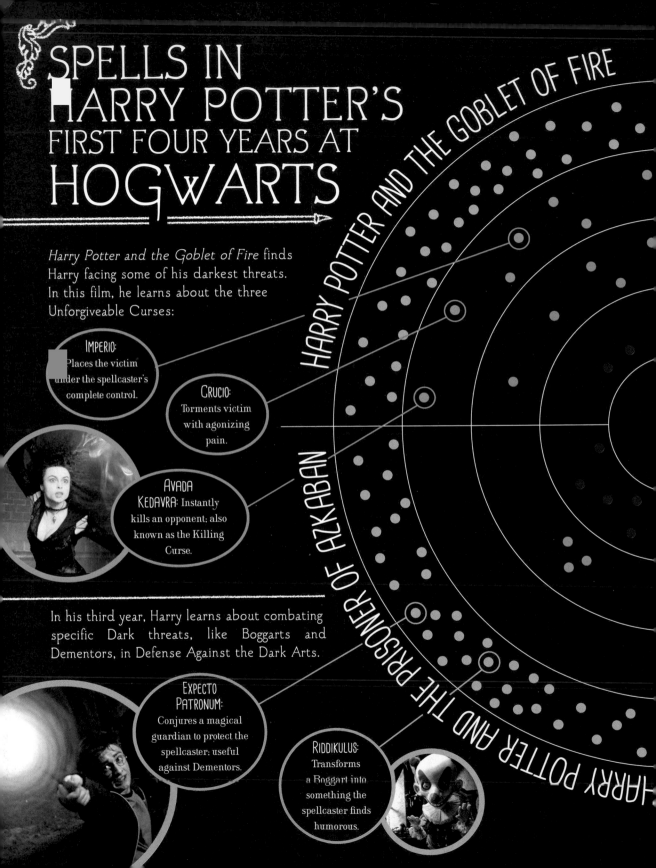

Harry Potter and the Goblet of Fire finds Harry facing some of his darkest threats. In this film, he learns about the three Unforgiveable Curses:

HARRY POTTER AND THE GOBLET OF FIRE

HARRY POTTER AND THE PRISONER OF AZKABAN

IMPERIO: Places the victim under the spellcaster's complete control.

CRUCIO: Torments victim with agonizing pain.

AVADA KEDAVRA: Instantly kills an opponent; also known as the Killing Curse.

In his third year, Harry learns about combating specific Dark threats, like Boggarts and Dementors, in Defense Against the Dark Arts.

EXPECTO PATRONUM: Conjures a magical guardian to protect the spellcaster; useful against Dementors.

RIDDIKULUS: Transforms a Boggart into something the spellcaster finds humorous.

SPELLS can be defensive or offensive, charm an object or curse an enemy. With a deep knowledge of magic, wizards and witches can even invent their own spells. In his first four years at Hogwarts, Harry learns a lot about the different types of magic and the basic spells needed to navigate the wizarding world.

CHARM

CURSE

TRANSFIGURATION

COUNTERSPELL

In *Harry Potter and the Sorcerer's Stone*, Hermione shines with her extensive study of *The Standard Book of Spells*.

ALOHOMORA: Opens doors and unlocks non-magical locks.

LACARNUM INFLAMARI: Shoots a fireball out the tip of one's wand.

PETRIFICUS TOTALUS: Freezes a victim in place.

Spells used in wizarding duels are introduced in *Harry Potter and the Chamber of Secrets*, as well as a handy spell to use against Acromantulas.

EXPELLIARMUS: Disarms an opponent.

SERPENSORTIA: Conjures a snake.

ARANIA EXUMAI: Blasts a spider backward.

HARRY POTTER AND THE CHAMBER OF SECRETS

- ● CHARMS
- ● CURSES
- ● TRANSFIGURATION
- ● COUNTERSPELLS

SPELLS IN HARRY'S LATER YEARS AT HOGWARTS AND BEYOND

Harry glimpses firsthand the incredible protection powers of magic in *Harry Potter and the Deathly Hallows–Part 2*, when professors and members of the Order of the Phoenix combine their powers to shield Hogwarts with powerful magic.

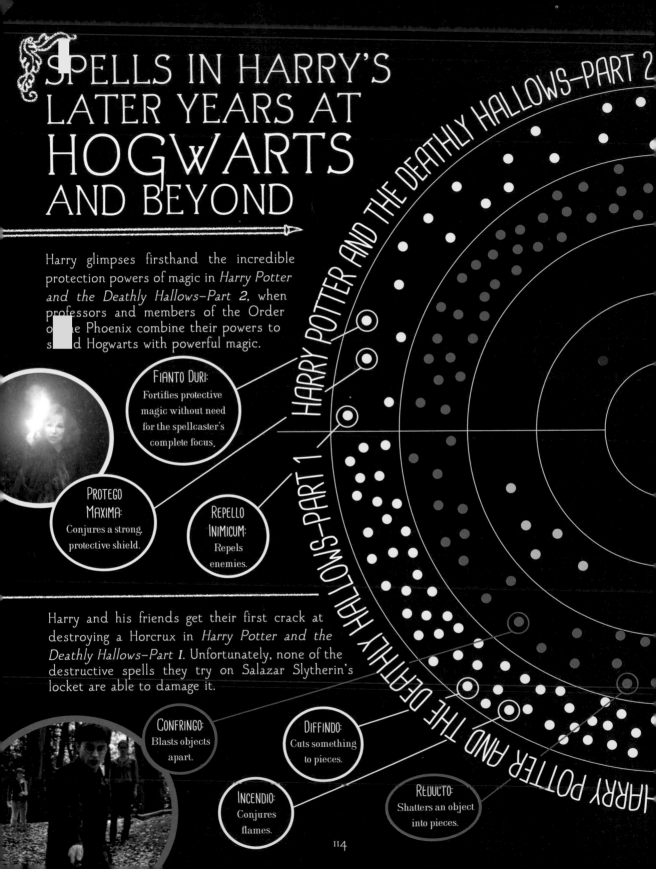

HARRY POTTER AND THE DEATHLY HALLOWS–PART 2

HARRY POTTER AND THE DEATHLY HALLOWS–PART 1

FIANTO DURI: Fortifies protective magic without need for the spellcaster's complete focus.

PROTEGO MAXIMA: Conjures a strong, protective shield.

REPELLO INIMICUM: Repels enemies.

Harry and his friends get their first crack at destroying a Horcrux in *Harry Potter and the Deathly Hallows–Part I*. Unfortunately, none of the destructive spells they try on Salazar Slytherin's locket are able to damage it.

CONFRINGO: Blasts objects apart.

DIFFINDO: Cuts something to pieces.

INCENDIO: Conjures flames.

REDUCTO: Shatters an object into pieces.

114

CHARM

CURSE

TRANSFIGURATION

In Harry's later years at Hogwarts and his entrance into the Second Wizarding War, he becomes entrenched in more complicated spells, as well as many spells for protection and defense. This knowledge serves his friends and himself later, when they find themselves on their own in a world dominated by Lord Voldemort.

In *Harry Potter and the Order of the Phoenix*, Harry and his friends take their Defense Against the Dark Arts education into their own hands, training as Dumbledore's Army.

LEVICORPUS:
Jinx that heaves victim into the air by their ankle.

STUPEFY:
Stuns an opponent.

INCARCEROUS:
Binds opponent with ropes.

HARRY POTTER AND THE HALF-BLOOD PRINCE

Things become even darker in Harry's sixth year, when he suspects and later confirms that his classmate Draco Malfoy has become one of Voldemort's Death Eaters.

OPPUGNO:
Jinx that commands an object or individual to attack a victim.

VULNERA SANENTUR:
Stops bleeding and heals wounds; useful countercurse to *Sectumsempra*

SECTUMSEMPRA:
Slashes a victim, causing extensive bleeding.

- CHARMS
- CURSES
- TRANSFIGURATION
- COUNTERSPELLS

SPELLS OF FANTASTIC BEASTS

A careful viewer will recognize many of the spells used by Harry Potter in the Fantastic Beasts films, but there are still many new spells to be learned here from Newt, Tina, Queenie, and Dumbledore.

Newt uses many different kinds of spells as he tracks down his lost creatures in *Fantastic Beasts and Where to Find Them*.

FINESTRA:
Shatters glass into dust.

LEGILIMENS:
Allows a skilled witch or wizard to read another person's thoughts, even over a far distance. Both Queenie and Snape are skilled in this art.

ABERTO:
Opens doors and portals.

FANTASTIC BEASTS AND WHERE TO FIND THEM

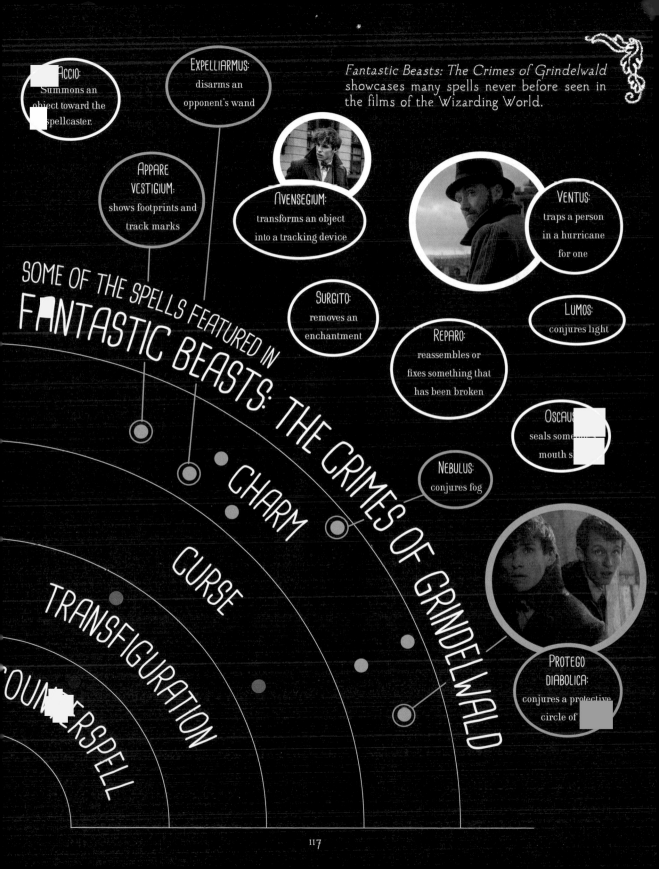

ACCIO: Summons an object toward the spellcaster.

EXPELLIARMUS: disarms an opponent's wand

APPARE VESTIGIUM: shows footprints and track marks

AVENSEGIUM: transforms an object into a tracking device

Fantastic Beasts: The Crimes of Grindelwald showcases many spells never before seen in the films of the Wizarding World.

VENTUS: traps a person in a hurricane for one

SURGITO: removes an enchantment

LUMOS: conjures light

REPARO: reassembles or fixes something that has been broken

OSCAUS seals some----- mouth s--

NEBULUS: conjures fog

PROTEGO DIABOLICA: conjures a protective circle of ----

SOME OF THE SPELLS FEATURED IN

FANTASTIC BEASTS: THE CRIMES OF GRINDELWALD

CHARM

CURSE

TRANSFIGURATION

COUNTERSPELL

UNDETECTABLE
EXTENSION CHARMS

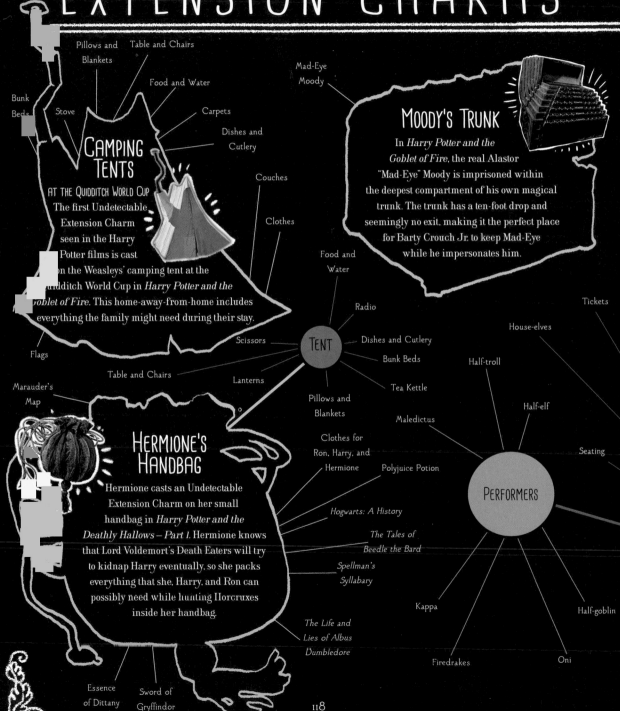

CAMPING TENTS

AT THE QUIDDITCH WORLD CUP

The first Undetectable Extension Charm seen in the Harry Potter films is cast on the Weasleys' camping tent at the Quidditch World Cup in *Harry Potter and the Goblet of Fire*. This home-away-from-home includes everything the family might need during their stay.

Pillows and Blankets
Table and Chairs
Food and Water
Bunk Beds
Stove
Carpets
Dishes and Cutlery
Couches
Clothes
Scissors
Flags
Table and Chairs
Lanterns

MOODY'S TRUNK

Mad-Eye Moody

In *Harry Potter and the Goblet of Fire*, the real Alastor "Mad-Eye" Moody is imprisoned within the deepest compartment of his own magical trunk. The trunk has a ten-foot drop and seemingly no exit, making it the perfect place for Barty Crouch Jr. to keep Mad-Eye while he impersonates him.

TENT

Food and Water
Radio
Dishes and Cutlery
Bunk Beds
Tea Kettle
Pillows and Blankets
Clothes for Ron, Harry, and Hermione
Maledictus
Polyjuice Potion

HERMIONE'S HANDBAG

Marauder's Map

Hermione casts an Undetectable Extension Charm on her small handbag in *Harry Potter and the Deathly Hallows – Part 1*. Hermione knows that Lord Voldemort's Death Eaters will try to kidnap Harry eventually, so she packs everything that she, Harry, and Ron can possibly need while hunting Horcruxes inside her handbag.

Hogwarts: A History
The Tales of Beedle the Bard
Spellman's Syllabary
The Life and Lies of Albus Dumbledore
Essence of Dittany
Sword of Gryffindor

PERFORMERS

Tickets
House-elves
Half-troll
Half-elf
Seating
Kappa
Half-goblin
Firedrakes
Oni

An **Undetectable Extension Charm** is an advanced piece of magic that allows the spellcaster to expand the internal dimensions of an object while keeping the external dimensions and weight of the object the same. (Essentially, an object becomes bigger on the inside than it appears on the outside.)

As Hermione confides in Harry, these charms are tricky to cast, but are used on a wide variety of objects, most commonly luggage and tents. Some of these charms (such as the one on Newt Scamander's case) are probably cast, shall we say, extralegally? It's not exactly legal to carry around a case full of magical, potentially dangerous creatures.

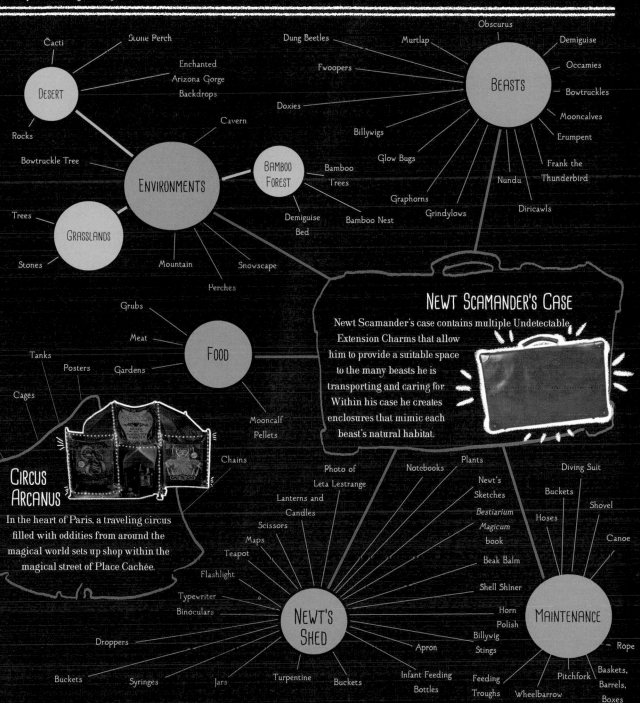

Desert
- Cacti
- Stone Perch
- Enchanted Arizona Gorge Backdrops
- Rocks

Environments
- Cavern

Bamboo Forest
- Bamboo Trees
- Bamboo Nest
- Demiguise Bed

Grasslands
- Bowtruckle Tree
- Trees
- Stones
- Mountain
- Snowscape
- Perches

Beasts
- Obscurus
- Murtlap
- Demiguise
- Occamies
- Bowtruckles
- Mooncalves
- Erumpent
- Frank the Thunderbird
- Diricawls
- Nundu
- Grindylows
- Graphorns
- Glow Bugs
- Billywigs
- Doxies
- Fwoopers
- Dung Beetles

Food
- Grubs
- Meat
- Gardens
- Mooncalf Pellets

Newt Scamander's Case

Newt Scamander's case contains multiple Undetectable Extension Charms that allow him to provide a suitable space to the many beasts he is transporting and caring for. Within his case he creates enclosures that mimic each beast's natural habitat.

Circus Arcanus

In the heart of Paris, a traveling circus filled with oddities from around the magical world sets up shop within the magical street of Place Cachée.
- Tanks
- Posters
- Cages
- Chains

Newt's Shed
- Photo of Leta Lestrange
- Notebooks
- Lanterns and Candles
- Scissors
- Maps
- Teapot
- Flashlight
- Typewriter
- Binoculars
- Droppers
- Buckets
- Syringes
- Jars
- Turpentine
- Buckets
- Apron
- Infant Feeding Bottles

Maintenance
- Plants
- Newt's Sketches
- *Bestiarium Magicum* book
- Beak Balm
- Shell Shiner
- Horn Polish
- Billywig Stings
- Diving Suit
- Buckets
- Hoses
- Shovel
- Canoe
- Rope
- Feeding Troughs
- Pitchfork
- Wheelbarrow
- Baskets, Barrels, Boxes

MAGICAL

POLYJUICE POTION

Drinking POLYJUICE POTION is a popular way to ALTER ONE'S APPEARANCE. Once the potion is brewed, the drinker need only add in something from the body of the other person, whether it be a fingernail, hair, or blood. The effects are usually temporary, lasting a few hours.

In *Harry Potter and the Chamber of Secrets*, Harry and Ron drink Polyjuice Potion to look like Slytherins Vincent Crabbe and Gregory Goyle, though notably the potion does not alter their voices.

Harry and his friends frequently drink Polyjuice Potion in the Second Wizarding War to disguise themselves. They use it to secretly transport Harry Potter to The Burrow to avoid Voldemort, to infiltrate the Ministry of Magic, and to break into Gringotts bank to gain one of the Horcruxes.

DISGUISES

In the films of the Wizarding World, things are not always as they appear. Magic can CAMOUFLAGE and CONCEAL, disguising not only APPEARANCE but also INTENT.

METAMORPHMAGUS

A rare number of wizards and witches can change their appearance at will. These Metamorphmagi seem to be naturally gifted with the ability from a young age.

NYMPHADORA TONKS is known to be a Metamorphmagus. She changes her hairstyle and facial features often throughout the Harry Potter films, even transforming her nose and mouth into a duck's bill over dinner during *Harry Potter and the Order of the Phoenix*.

TRANSFIGURATION

Transfiguration spells are for advanced witches and wizards capable of rearranging their physical form to alter their appearance. This magic is difficult to master, but its effectiveness is long-lasting and almost impossible to detect.

During his time in New York, GELLERT GRINDELWALD Transfigures himself into PERCIVAL GRAVES, MACUSA's Director of Magical Security. It isn't until Newt casts *Revelio* on him at the end of *Fantastic Beasts and Where to Find Them* that his true face is revealed.

PROPHECIES

TRELAWNEY'S PROPHECIES

Professor Sybill Trelawney, who teaches Divination at Hogwarts, has made prophecies that some interpret to signify the conflict between Lord Voldemort and Harry Potter. In *Harry Potter and the Prisoner of Azkaban*, she observes that Harry has "the Grim"–an omen of death–and accurately predicts the return of Peter Pettigrew and the deaths of Sirius Black and Buckbeak: "He will return tonight. Tonight, he who betrayed his friends, whose heart rots with murder shall break free. Innocent blood shall be spilt, and servant and master shall be reunited once more."

But Trelawney's most startling prediction is one from before Harry's birth, one that Harry discovered in *Harry Potter and the Order of the Phoenix*: "The one with the power to vanquish the Dark Lord approaches . . . And the Dark Lord shall mark him as his equal, but he shall have power the Dark Lord knows not. For neither can live while the other survives."

Those gifted in the arts of DIVINATION have made predictions and prophecies for many centuries. Whenever a major moment in wizarding history occurs, there are often prophecies to go along with it.

SOUL SEARCH

While trying to find the Obscurus in New York, Percival Graves befriends Credence and tells the young man of a vision he had:

"My vision showed only the child's immense power. He or she is no older than ten, and I saw this child in close proximity to your mother—she I saw so plainly. There is something else. Something I haven't told you. I saw you beside me in New York. You're the one that gains this child's trust. You are the key—I saw this. You want to join the wizarding world. I want those things, too, Credence. I want them for you. So find the child. Find the child and we'll all be free."

PROPHECY KEEPERS: The Department of Mysteries at the Ministry of Magic retains recorded prophecies, but only the subject of the prophecy may retrieve it.

Herbology

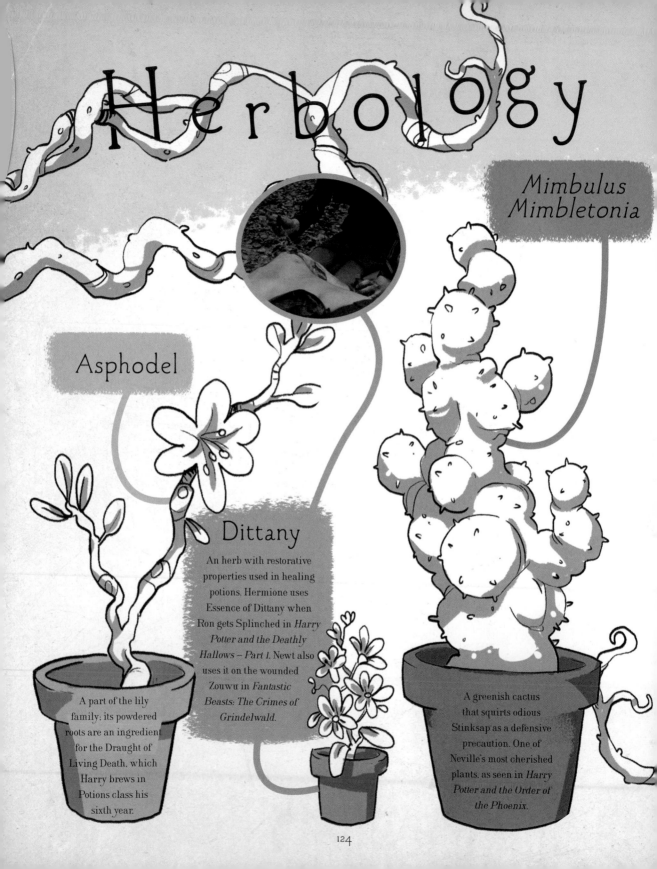

Mimbulus Mimbletonia

Asphodel

A part of the lily family; its powdered roots are an ingredient for the Draught of Living Death, which Harry brews in Potions class his sixth year.

Dittany

An herb with restorative properties used in healing potions. Hermione uses Essence of Dittany when Ron gets Splinched in *Harry Potter and the Deathly Hallows – Part 1*. Newt also uses it on the wounded Zouwu in *Fantastic Beasts: The Crimes of Grindelwald*.

A greenish cactus that squirts odious Stinksap as a defensive precaution. One of Neville's most cherished plants, as seen in *Harry Potter and the Order of the Phoenix*.

FLORA is as magical as fauna, though it seems magical beasts make more news than plants and fungi. Yet for dedicated Herbologists, the BOTANICAL LIFE they care for is far more astounding than anything that walks or growls.

Mandrake

A plant with roots that looks like a human figure, used in a restorative draught to resuscitate the Petrified victims of the Basilisk in Harry's second year.

Gillyweed

When consumed, Gillyweed endows the eater with gills to breathe underwater that last for about an hour. Harry uses Gillyweed during the second task of the Triwizard Tournament in *Harry Potter and the Goblet of Fire*.

Devil's Snare

A creeper plant that, when touched, constricts and strangles that which touched it. A rhyme from Hermione's Herbology book specifies its weakness: "Devil's Snare is deadly fun, but will sulk in the sun."

POTIONS

To put it simply, POTIONS are BOTTLED MAGIC. Each substance, when properly brewed, produces a prescribed magical effect on those who imbibe or apply it. Using them is easy; brewing them, on the other hand, requires concentration, exactitude, special ingredients, and much patience.

AMORTENTIA

Drinker experiences intense infatuation and passion for the one who gives it. These are sold at Weasleys' Wizard Wheezes and smell differently to each person. To Hermione, it smells of "freshly-mown grass and new parchment and spearmint toothpaste."

DRAUGHT OF LIVING DEATH

Induces a deep slumber that resembles death. Harry successfully brews it in *Harry Potter and the Half-Blood Prince* with the help of his annotated *Advanced Potion-Making* textbook.

POLYJUICE POTION

Transforms the drinker's appearance into that of another person.

FELIX FELICIS

Bestows the drinker with amazing luck.

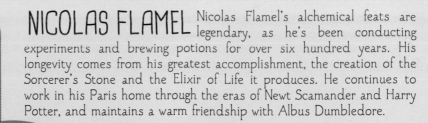

NICOLAS FLAMEL

Nicolas Flamel's alchemical feats are legendary, as he's been conducting experiments and brewing potions for over six hundred years. His longevity comes from his greatest accomplishment, the creation of the Sorcerer's Stone and the Elixir of Life it produces. He continues to work in his Paris home through the eras of Newt Scamander and Harry Potter, and maintains a warm friendship with Albus Dumbledore.

ANTIDOTES

The BEZOAR can act as an antidote to most poisons. Harry uses it to save Ron from a poisoned bottle of mead in *Harry Potter and the Half-Blood Prince*.

"REGROWING BONES IS A NASTY BUSINESS."

SKELE-GRO

Regrows vanished bones. Madam Pomfrey administered this potion to Harry in *Harry Potter and the Chamber of Secrets*. After Harry broke his arm in a Quidditch match, Professor Lockhart attempted to fix it, but he accidentally made all of Harry's arm bones vanish instead!

VERITASERUM

Makes the drinker tell the truth. Dolores Umbridge forces Severus Snape to brew it so she can interrogate students during Harry's fifth year.

ELIXIR OF LIFE

Produced from the Sorcerer's Stone to extend the drinker's life. Nicholas Flamel, the noted alchemist, has brewed it to lengthen his life.

MURTLAP ESSENCE

Accelerates the healing process of wounds, as explained by Newt Scamander in *Fantastic Beasts and Where to Find Them*.

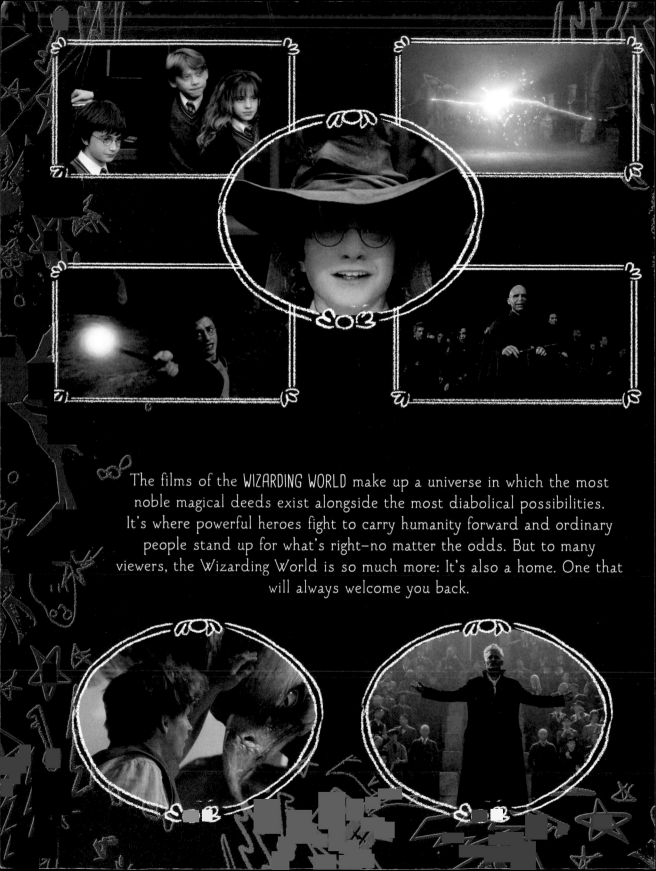

The films of the WIZARDING WORLD make up a universe in which the most noble magical deeds exist alongside the most diabolical possibilities. It's where powerful heroes fight to carry humanity forward and ordinary people stand up for what's right—no matter the odds. But to many viewers, the Wizarding World is so much more: It's also a home. One that will always welcome you back.